SPIDER-MAN

INTO THE SPIDER-VERSE

The Junior Novel

© 2018 MARVEL © 2018 SPA & CPII

Little, Brown and Company
Hachette Book Group
1290 Avenue of the Americas, New York, NY 10104
Visit us at LBYR.com

First Edition: December 2018

Little, Brown and Company is a division of Hachette Book Group, Inc.
The Little, Brown name and logo are trademarks of Hachette Book Group, Inc.

The publisher is not responsible for websites (or their content)
that are not owned by the publisher.

Library of Congress Control Number: 2018959654

ISBNs: 978-0-316-48028-4 (pbk.), 978-0-316-48027-7 (ebook)

Printed in the United States of America

LSC-C

10 9 8 7 6 5 4 3 2 1

SPIDER-MAN

INTO THE SPIDER-VERSE

The Junior Novel

Adapted by
Steve Behling

Little, Brown and Company
New York Boston

CHAPTER 1

The best thing about headphones?

When you wear 'em, the rest of the world doesn't exist. Nothing else exists except you and your music.

The worst thing about headphones?

You have to take 'em off sometime.

"Miles! Miles!"

Whipping off his headphones, Miles Morales heard his dad calling his name. He was sitting at the small desk in his bedroom, drawing, listening to music. Carefree, not a worry to his name.

Well, that wasn't entirely true.

"Yeah?" Miles shouted at the door.

"Are you finished packing for school?"

"Yeah!" Miles hollered back. That was the general all-purpose answer when his parents asked him if he had done something yet—*YEAH*. It saved a lot of yelling. Then he added, "Just going back over my list!"

Looking down at the floor, Miles saw his empty suitcase and his backpack. Then he leaped into action. He opened his dresser drawers one at a time, grabbing various items he would need—socks, underwear, T-shirts, shorts. He tossed them into the suitcase.

Darting over to his closet, he pulled a few shirts and some pants off a small wire rack inside. Toss.

Then the blue uniform jacket for his new school.

My new school, Miles thought. *Wish it was my* old *school.* He threw the uniform into the suitcase, then slammed the lid shut. He stuffed a few books into his backpack, along with his drawing pad and a case full of pencils, pens, and erasers. He zipped it up.

"Miles!"

Uh-oh, Miles realized. *Mom.*

When his mom yelled, it was all over. Miles picked up his backpack and suitcase and ran down the hallway to the living room.

"Where's my laptop?" Miles asked, out of breath.

"Where'd you last put it?" Miles's mom, Rio, asked. It was a question she asked her son at least fifty times a day.

Miles rooted around the living room, trying to find the laptop. It was a prerequisite for school—there was no way he could get along without it.

How does a laptop just disappear?

Miles's dad, Jefferson, stood by the front door, dangling his car keys. "If you want me to drive you, we gotta go now . . ." he said.

Miles didn't look up from his search. "No, Dad, I'll walk!" he protested.

"Personal chauffeur going once . . ."

"It's okay!" Miles said again, trying to drive home the point that he really didn't want to get a ride with his dad. Not in the first few weeks of school.

Rio stared at Miles, shaking her head. "¡Ay Maria, este nene me tiene loca!"

At last, Miles swatted away a bunch of magazines on the coffee table and found the laptop underneath. Tucking the computer under his arm, he reached for the quick, on-the-go breakfast his mom had made for him. He shoved the toast into his mouth and tried to remember to chew with his mouth closed, with limited success.

"Miles, gotta go!" Rio said, insistent.

"In a minute!" Miles replied, mouth full of food.

"Gotta go-oh . . ." Rio said in a singsong voice.

"IN A MINUTE!" Miles said, raising his voice reflexively.

Rio rolled her eyes, an amused smile on her face, unaffected by her son's outburst.

Miles finished chewing, gathered up his suitcase, stuffed his laptop into his backpack, and raced out the door.

"Mom, I gotta go!" Miles said. He was standing on the stoop of his apartment, trying to break free of his mother's embrace. The embrace that threatened to squash him like a bug. She was hugging him and showering him with kisses. It was at once embarrassing and awesome. Miles knew how much his mother loved him.

"In a minute," Rio said, still kissing her son's cheeks.

Miles put his suitcase on the ground and rolled the wheels down the steps from his apartment to the street.

"Papá! Llámame, okay?" Rio shouted, a sad smile on her face.

"Sí, claro, Mama. ¡Adiós!" Miles shouted.

Away from his apartment at last, Miles made his way down the early-morning Brooklyn street. He'd have to hurry if he was going to make it to his new school on time. He wasn't making good time. The suitcase was cumbersome, and the backpack was really heavy.

Maybe I should have packed a little more carefully, Miles thought.

"*Ohhhh.* Look who's back! Yo, what's going on, bro?"

Miles snapped to and looked up. He realized he was walking right past Brooklyn Middle School, where he had gone the last few years. His friend Laszlo was standing outside on the sidewalk, and he waved to Miles.

"Hey, I'm just walking by, how you doing?" Miles said, smiling. He was glad to see Laszlo, and more than a little sad that they wouldn't get to hang out at school this year.

"You keepin' 'em on their toes, Miles?" asked Domingo, another friend.

"You know I'm trying," Miles replied, trying to sound cool.

"Look who it is! Nice uniform!" another kid interjected. It was that kid whose name Miles could never remember. He felt kind of bad about that.

Miles nodded. "Hey, they make me wear it, all right?" He gestured with his right hand at the school uniform he was wearing. It made him feel uncomfortable, and he was pretty self-conscious about it.

A girl ran up from the schoolyard, squeezing in between Laszlo and Domingo. "Just gonna walk away? We miss you, Miles!" she said, her face sincere.

"You miss me?" Miles replied. "I still live here! Wait, you miss me?"

The bell rang, and the kids threw a collective wave at Miles. Miles waved back, then watched as they ran through the schoolyard and into the building.

It was pretty sad, just watching it. Miles missed his old friends already. With a sigh, he grabbed his things and continued down the street.

Reaching into his backpack, Miles fished out a couple stickers that he'd been working on. Some cool designs that he'd come up with overnight. Drawing was a great release for him. It let him work out all kinds of thoughts and feelings on paper. But the best part? Walking around town and slapping his art in places where people could see his work. He peeled the backing off one sticker and smashed it on the side of a mailbox. Then he took another and slapped it on a stop sign with a loud *clang*.

He took a few steps, crossing the street, then stumbled. Before he could even pick himself up off the pavement, he saw flashing lights and heard the *BWOOP BWOOP* of a police siren.

Oh, c'mon, he thought.

"Seriously, Dad, walking would have been fine," Miles said, sitting in the back seat of his father's police cruiser. Jefferson was listening to the news on the radio, and the sound filled the back seat as well.

"You can walk plenty on Saturday when you peel those stickers off," Jefferson chided Miles, talking over the voice of the newscaster.

"You saw that?" Miles said playfully. "I don't know if that was me, Dad."

"And the two from yesterday on Clinton," Jefferson replied.

Dang, Miles thought. *Can't get anything past him.*

"Okay, yeah . . . those were me," Miles admitted.

Miles looked forward and saw his dad glaring at him in the rearview mirror. The look said it all: *DON'T MESS WITH ME.* Miles sighed and slumped down in his seat, watching the buildings move by as he stared out the window. They passed coffee shop after coffee shop, and Miles had to wonder just how much coffee people could actually drink.

"*Soooo,*" his father said, trying to make conversation. "Look at that, another new coffee shop. You see that, Miles?"

"Yep, I see it," Miles said, disinterested.

"You see that one, what's that one called?" Jefferson said, pointing out his window.

"Foam Party," Miles said, sounding bored.

"Foam Party, come on," Jefferson said. "And everyone is just lining up! You see that, Miles?"

"I see it," Miles replied.

"Is that a coffee shop or a disco?" Jefferson said, trying to crack a joke.

"Dad, you're old, man," Miles said flatly. He slumped even deeper in his seat as he turned his attention to the news broadcast.

"This is the second earthquake this month, but lucky for these folks, Spider-Man was there to save the day!" said the newscaster.

Jefferson shook his head, then punched a button on the dashboard, turning off the radio.

Oh man, here it comes, Miles thought.

"Spider-Man," Jefferson railed. "I mean, this guy swings in once a day, *zip-zap-zop*, in his little mask, and answers to no one, right?"

"Yeah, Dad," Miles sighed.

"And meanwhile, my guys are out there, lives on the line—"

"Uh-huh," Miles said, nonplussed. He had heard it all a thousand times before. Probably more than a thousand. His dad hated Spider-Man. So what? Big deal.

Miles looked out the window of the police car and saw that some schoolkids were running right alongside. Miles sank into his seat as one of them hit the window and mouthed, *You get arrested?*

I definitely should have walked, Miles thought.

"—and no masks!" Jefferson continued, still on his Spider-Man rant. "We show our faces. Accountability!"

"Dad, speed up, I know these kids. . . ." Miles pleaded.

But Jefferson was too wrapped up in his diatribe to notice. "You know, with great ability comes great accountability," he said.

"That's not how the saying goes, Dad," Miles corrected. "It's a yellow light!"

"I do like his cereal, though," Jefferson said magnanimously. "I'll give him that." Then he slammed the brakes on the car.

Miles was flung against the divider between the front and back seats. "Oh my gosh!" he exclaimed. "Don't cops run red lights?"

"Some do," Jefferson said. "But not your dad!"

CHAPTER 2

"**Y**ou going in?"

Miles sat in the back of his dad's police cruiser, not wanting to get out but knowing he had to.

"Dad," Miles said, trying not to whine but failing. "Why can't I go back to Brooklyn Middle?"

He wasn't sure why he was choosing now to have this conversation that they'd already had a million times, especially now that he'd started school at Visions. But Miles just had to keep trying.

Jefferson sighed. "Miles, you've given it two weeks," he said, staring out the front window at the students walking across the street. "We're not having this conversation."

I knew he was gonna say that, Miles thought.

"I just think this new school is elitist," Miles said, dragging out his losing argument. "And I would prefer to be at a normal school among the people."

"The *people*?" Jefferson said, his voice and his temper raising. "These *are* your people!"

"I'm only here 'cause I won that stupid lottery," Miles moped.

"No way," Jefferson said, putting a stop to Miles's protest. "You passed the entry test just like everybody else. You have an opportunity here. You wanna blow that, huh? You want to end up like your uncle?"

"Uncle Aaron is a good guy," Miles muttered under his breath.

"We all make choices in life," Jefferson said, shaking his head.

"Doesn't feel like I have a choice!" Miles volleyed back.

"You don't!" Jefferson roared, the tone of his voice final and absolute.

Miles sighed and pushed open the door. He started to get out of the car.

It's hopeless, he thought.

"Look," Jefferson said, slightly calmer. "I know it's hard during the week being away from Mom and me−"

Sticking his head back into the car, Miles said, "Actually,

that part's great. I love that part." He smiled at his dad, trying to lighten the mood with his joke.

His dad just stared at him.

Ugh.

Miles stepped back and slammed the door. Then he opened the passenger door and got his suitcase.

"I love you, Miles," Jefferson said, seeming at a loss for words.

"Yeah, I know, Dad," Miles said. "See you Friday."

Then he shut the door and walked away from the police cruiser. He knew his dad was watching him, but Miles didn't turn around.

A burst of static cut through the air, and Miles cringed.

"You gotta say *I love you* back," Jefferson boomed over the cruiser's PA system.

The students who had been milling about outside Visions Academy all turned to look in Miles's direction.

"Dad, are you serious?" Miles felt his face flush red.

"I wanna hear it," Jefferson replied.

"You wanna hear me say—"

"*I love you, Dad.*" Jefferson's voice crackled, still on the PA, as he completed the sentence.

"You're dropping me off at school!" Miles protested.

"*I love you, Dad,*" Jefferson repeated.

"Look at this place," Miles said, noting the presence of all the other students and the incredibly embarrassing nature of the whole situation.

"Dad, I love you."

Miles sighed, knowing there was no way he could win this battle and keep even a shred of dignity. "Dad, I love you," Miles said loudly, if somewhat grudgingly.

"That's a copy," Jefferson thundered over the PA. "Tie your shoes, please!"

As Miles entered the lobby of Visions Academy, he looked down at his feet. Sure enough, his shoes were untied. He gave them a quick once-over, and then, out of spite, just left them alone.

Serve him right if I trip, Miles thought.

All around him, Miles saw kids wearing the same blue uniforms. They all seemed to be taller than him. He walked past a wall of photographs, all pictures of the donors and corporations that had contributed money to keep Visions Academy up and running. He saw a picture of Wilson Fisk, one of the biggest businessmen in New York City. His company, Fisk Industries, underwrote much of Visions' budget. And there was Alchemax, a company that held so many patents that Miles couldn't keep track of them all.

"*I love you, Dad!*"

Miles whirled around to see a big uniformed kid sneering in his face.

Great, Miles thought. *He saw the whole thing with Dad. Now I'm gonna be the* I love you *kid for the rest of my life.*

Then he took a deep breath and decided he wasn't going to let any of that derail his day.

All right, Miles. Let's give this another shot.

"Hey, good morning!" Miles said, flagging down another student. "How you doing? Weekend was short, huh?"

"*That's a copy!*" the student responded.

Ugh, Miles moaned internally.

Miles moved on, extricating himself from any more embarrassment. He looked around and saw all the kids hurrying about their day. They just seemed to keep right on going, as if Miles weren't even there.

Everyone seemed so serious at Visions. Not like Brooklyn Middle. At Brooklyn Middle, the kids knew how to have fun.

"Hey!"

Miles snapped to attention when he heard a student's voice. "Yeah?" he said, hopeful that someone might finally want to have a normal conversation.

"Your shoes are untied," the student said, pointing at Miles's feet.

Miles looked down, saw his laces dangling on the floor, and sighed. "I'm aware," he said, as the student rushed off. "It's a choice."

CHAPTER 3

From that moment on, the day was a blur of classes. Miles went from one room to another, inundated by an ever-changing group of students and teachers. From math to logic, from literature to chemistry, Miles's brain was being overloaded with new concepts.

And his backpack was being overloaded with homework. It seemed to Miles that the amount of papers and books that he accumulated throughout the day was directly proportional to the number of classes he attended.

At this rate, I'm gonna be buried, Miles thought.

He was tired, stressed, and generally unhappy with his situation. Miles wished again that he could be back at Brooklyn Middle right now, instead of sitting in Ms. Calleros's class.

Ms. Calleros's class? Oh man. I'm late!

Miles bolted down the hallway. He'd been so wrapped up in thought that he hadn't even realized the bell had already rung. He rounded a corner, holding his backpack to make sure it didn't fly off his shoulder. He made it to Ms. Calleros's room and threw open the door. The room was dark, and Miles thought for a second that maybe he wasn't late—maybe he was the first one there?

Then the lights flicked on, and Ms. Calleros said, "You're late, Mr. Morales."

That knocked out what little air was left in Miles's sails. "Einstein said time was relative, right?" he said, trying to worm his way out of the situation. "Maybe I'm not late. Maybe you guys are early."

Ms. Calleros didn't smile. She didn't laugh. She didn't even respond. Miles looked around the classroom. No one else seemed to find his comment very funny, either, except for one girl, who laughed a little.

"Sorry," the girl said, covering up her smile. "It was just so quiet."

"Sit down," Ms. Calleros said, turning her attention away from Miles and heading back to the front of the classroom. A student turned the lights off, and Miles started making his way to his seat in the dark, smacking into the furniture along the way.

On the whiteboard at the front of the room, a documentary started. Miles saw a title appear beneath the image of a woman in a lab coat. It said, DIRECTOR, ALCHEMAX LABORATORIES. Pausing, Miles watched as the woman tried to excite her audience.

"Our universe is in fact one of many parallel universes happening at the exact same time. Thanks to everyone here at the Fisk Family Foundation for the Sciences, I will prove they exist when I build my supercollider. All I need is ten billion dollars! Chump change, right? And who knows . . . maybe we'll find other people just like us!"

Miles watched the documentary, still bonking into furniture on the way to his seat. He really was interested in the subject matter, but the documentary seemed to be more of a promotional film for Alchemax than anything else. There were many shots of the woman wearing a hard hat and riding around an Alchemax facility in a golf cart, or standing around with other people wearing lab coatsand "doing science."

Ouch!

Miles felt his right shin smack into a desk and, as he bent down to rub it, saw that the desk belonged to the girl who had laughed at his joke. She was new. Well, newer than he was. He sat down next to her and watched her watch the documentary.

Then she looked at Miles. Busted. Miles turned away, pretending he hadn't been staring in the first place. But when he looked back, he saw that the new girl was still staring at him.

"I liked your joke," she whispered. "I mean, it wasn't funny–that's why I laughed–but it was smart, so I liked it."

"I don't think I've seen you before," Miles said, trying to keep his voice down.

"*Shhhhh!*" Ms. Calleros said, suddenly behind Miles.

How does she do that? he wondered.

"After class, Mr. Morales," she said, and Miles knew he was in for it. He tried to turn his attention back to the documentary, but he was preoccupied with the new girl sitting next to him.

"Every choice we make would create countless possible futures," the woman in the documentary continued. "A 'What if' to infinity . . ."

Countless other possibilities? Miles thought. *That means there could be, like, countless other Mileses out there right now. Weird.*

"A zero," Ms. Calleros said, her voice full of disappointment.

Miles sat across from Ms. Calleros, who showed him a piece of paper. The paper happened to be the latest quiz, and it had a big *0%* written on it in red ink.

The quiz belonged to Miles.

"A zero," Miles said, momentarily at a loss for words. He furrowed his brow but then let out a small sigh of relief. "Few more of those, you'd probably have to kick me out of here, huh? Maybe I'm just not right for this school."

Ms. Calleros shifted in her seat, never taking her eyes off Miles. "If a person wearing a blindfold picked the answers on a true-or-false quiz at random, do you know what score they would get?"

"*Uhh,* fifty percent," Miles said. Then it dawned on him. "Wait—"

The teacher smiled and nodded. "That's right!" she said. "Very sharp! On a true-or false quiz, the only way to get all the answers wrong is to know which answers are right."

Then Miles watched as Ms. Calleros reached into a drawer, grabbed a red pen, and changed the *0%* on the quiz to a *100%.*

Miles felt his stomach drop and fumbled to say something, anything. "Or . . . or it's a statistical aberration," he started. "I mean, at the far end—"

"You're a very clever guy, Miles," Ms. Calleros interrupted. She folded her hands together and leaned over the desk. "But I know what you're doing. No one is kicking you out of this school. I want you to start keeping a journal. I'll start reviewing it each week. And I want you to write about what you want your future to be."

Miles slumped into his seat in defeat. *So much for getting kicked out and going back to Brooklyn Middle.*

CHAPTER 4

One look at the stack of homework piled high on his desk, and Miles felt like disappearing. Going anywhere, doing anything, would be better than trying to sort through that mess. He thumped the eraser end of a pencil against his lips and stared at the piece of paper.

The essay was due tomorrow, and he'd barely gotten as far as the title.

The universe hates me, he thought.

Swiveling away from his desk, he saw his roommate, Ganke, reading a comic book, with headphones on. Miles could hear the music blasting from them. He didn't want to interrupt, but Miles also really needed a break.

"Hey!" he said, trying to get Ganke's attention. "You finish your homework already?"

Ganke didn't say anything. He didn't even look up. He just sat there, thumbing through the comic, rubbing the few hairs that sat above his upper lip.

I guess it's a mustache, Miles thought. *Kinda. Sorta.*

"I'm your roommate, Miles," he continued. "Who you've lived with for two weeks and barely spoken to?"

Nothing.

"Kinda like I'm invisible, right? All right, cool. Good convo," Miles finished. Then he swiveled back to his desk, shaking his head as he stared at the dreaded piece of paper. With a sigh, he looked out the dorm room window.

And then Miles Morales had an idea.

Miles was on the fire escape, peering in through an apartment window on the top floor. A guy was sitting on his couch, phone in hand, texting. So Miles took a picture of the guy with his phone.

And he texted it to the guy on the couch.

Miles could barely contain his laughter as he saw the guy look at his phone, and his face light up in a grin. The guy peered around the room and raced to the window. Miles pressed his face against the glass, pulling a silly face.

Uncle Aaron yanked open the window. "Get inside,"

he said, chuckling. Miles ducked through the opening as his uncle moved to the sink.

"Speak up, Nephew. You know I can't hear you when I'm washing the dishes," Uncle Aaron said as he scrubbed a pot.

"Yeah, I hear the ears are the first thing to go," Miles said. He walked to his uncle's punching bag and took a few shots at it. It felt awkward.

"I heard *that*," Uncle Aaron said. "I'm all good, my man. What's up with school?"

Miles shrugged and tagged the bag with his left hand, then his right. "Six hours of homework a night. When am I supposed to sleep, huh?" he said.

"You can't tell me it's all that bad there," Uncle Aaron replied as he placed the pot in the rack next to the sink. "Smart girls is where it's at. Place must be full of 'em." He walked over to the punching bag and held it with his hands, putting his body behind it.

"C'mon, man, c'mon," he said, inviting Miles to take a shot at the bag.

"No, there's no one," Miles replied. "There's no one."

Uncle Aaron raised a skeptical eyebrow, then released the bag. He walked over to the microwave and grabbed a box of popcorn sitting on top. He took out a bag, ripped open the plastic, and set the paper popcorn bag inside the microwave.

"C'mon, man," Uncle Aaron said again, closing the microwave door and pressing the START button. "I cannot have a nephew of mine on the streets with no game."

"I got game!" Miles said defensively. "There was this new girl, actually, she's kinda into me. You know how it is."

"What's her name?" Uncle Aaron asked.

Miles took a seat on the couch and picked up the notebook he'd brought with him. He started to sketch while he talked. "You know we . . ." Miles mumbled. "This is . . . We're laying the groundwork right now."

Uncle Aaron looked at Miles and smiled a little. "You know about the shoulder touch?"

"Of course I do!" Miles said. *No, I don't.* "But tell me anyway."

"Tomorrow," Uncle Aaron said, "find that girl, walk up to her, and be like, *Hey.*" Then he pretended to touch an imaginary shoulder. "I'm telling you, man, it's science."

"You serious, Uncle Aaron?" Miles asked. "So, walk up to her and be like . . . *Hey.*"

Uncle Aaron started to laugh. "No, no, no, no . . . like, *Hey,*" he said, sounding a million times cooler than Miles had saying the same word two seconds ago.

"*Hey,*" Miles tried again.

Uncle Aaron shook his head. "No. *Heyyy.*"

"*Heyyyy.*"

"You sure you're my nephew, man?" Uncle Aaron joked.

Miles felt the phone in his pocket vibrate.

"Is that her?" Uncle Aaron teased.

I don't think so. . . .

Miles stared at the phone screen and saw an incoming text from his dad: *Finish that homework?*

"I should go," Miles said reluctantly. "Still got a paper to do tonight."

If Uncle Aaron had been paying attention and heard his nephew, he didn't let on. Instead, he walked over to the couch and looked at the notebook Miles had been scribbling in just a few minutes earlier.

"Yo, you've been holding out on me. You throw these up yet?" Uncle Aaron said, checking out Miles's designs.

"No, you know my dad," Miles replied. "I can't."

"Come on," Uncle Aaron said. "I got a spot you will not believe."

"I can't!" Miles protested. "I can't, I can't, I can't . . ."

"I'm gonna get in so much trouble!"

The subway tunnel was dark and dank. Miles could smell about fifty different odors wafting down the tube, and none of them were good.

What was he doing down here with his uncle? He really did have homework to do! His parents would kill him if they found out he'd left campus to go hang out with his uncle in the subway tunnels. And they'd really flip if they knew what they were up to.

"Hey, man," Uncle Aaron said. "Tell them your art teacher made you."

They walked a little farther, until they came to a large metal fence stretching from the ground almost to the ceiling. Miles saw a sign that said ALCHEMAX—PRIVATE PROPERTY.

Someone really doesn't want anyone around here, Miles thought.

With grace, Uncle Aaron climbed right up the fence and dropped down to the other side. He motioned for Miles to follow.

If I get caught I am so dead.

Miles climbed up the fence, not quite as gracefully as his uncle, and landed with a *thud* next to him.

CHAPTER 5

The darkened subway tunnel seemed to go on forever. Full of spiderwebs. They seemed to cover all the walls as far as Miles could see.

It was like some huge, weird, creepy cavern.

"Whoa," Miles heard himself say out loud. He looked at the enormous space, and then, at the top of his lungs, yelled, "*Brooklyn!*"

Then he heard "Brooklyn!" echo for the next couple of seconds.

Uncle Aaron tugged at Miles's shirt, motioning for him to follow. Miles did, and as they walked along the tunnel, Miles saw something else.

Miles couldn't believe what he was looking at. A huge tunnel wall, tagged by who knows how many artists. It was like the world's largest canvas, and it was just waiting for others to come along and add their story.

"There's a lot of history on these walls," Uncle Aaron said, his voice full of respect.

"This is so fresh!" Miles said in disbelief.

Uncle Aaron leaned down and opened the bag he had slung over his shoulder. He pulled out a few cans of spray paint and tossed one over to his nephew. Then he set out a small boom box and hit PLAY.

The tunes echoed in the subway tunnel as uncle and nephew, fellow artists, went to work.

"Now you're on your own, Miles," Uncle Aaron said as he started to paint. "Whoa, slow down a little."

Miles had been moving his spray can quickly across the concrete wall. Listening to his uncle, he slowed the motion of his hand.

"That's better," Uncle Aaron observed. "That's perfect."

Miles always enjoyed the time he spent with his uncle. Even if his father didn't seem to think too much of it.

He was wholly absorbed in the process, lost in a world of his own making. Miles just went with the feeling, pouring himself into each press of the nozzle.

He was so into what he was doing that he didn't notice it. Faint. Glowing.

A spider.

So tiny it escaped notice. It descended from the ceiling, dropping slowly, slowly, on a thin strand of webbing. At last, it dropped from its web and landed in the pile of spray cans Uncle Aaron had set on the ground.

"That's it," Uncle Aaron said, admiring his nephew's handiwork. "Now you can cut that line with another color. That's it . . . yeah, that's it!"

Miles had found his groove and was thoroughly enjoying himself. He gazed upward and saw a part of the wall he wanted to paint, but it was too high. "A little help?" he said, gesturing to his uncle.

Without hesitation, Uncle Aaron picked up his nephew and whisked Miles up to his shoulders. Miles was able to reach the area he wanted to paint.

"You want drips? 'Cause if you do, that's cool, but if you don't you gotta keep it moving." He showed Miles what he meant by using his own paint can to demonstrate.

"That's intentional!" Miles said, referring to the drips in his painting.

They're so *not intentional*, he thought.

A few seconds later, Miles had finished, and he jumped off Uncle Aaron's shoulders. Together, they stepped back to take a look at the mural they had been painting.

"Wow," Uncle Aaron said.

30

Miles stared at the painting, a little unsure. "Is it too crazy?" he asked.

Uncle Aaron shook his head. "No, man. Miles . . ." he began. "I see exactly what you're doing here, man."

Miles smiled at his uncle.

"Yeah," Uncle Aaron said. "Me and your dad, we used to tag all the time back in the day."

"Stop lying," Miles replied.

There is no way Dad would ever have anything to do with a place like this, he thought.

"It's true," Uncle Aaron said. "Then he took on the cop thing . . . and I don't know. He's a good guy, it's just . . . You know what I'm saying?"

The conversation was interrupted by the vibrating of Uncle Aaron's phone. He took a look at the screen, then pocketed the phone.

"All right, come on, man. I gotta roll," he said to his nephew. He gathered up their painting supplies and walked out of the tunnel.

For a moment, Miles was alone. He took a step back and admired the work that he and his uncle had done that night.

That feels so right, he thought.

He got out his phone to take a picture of their masterpiece.

He didn't see the spider until it was too late.

CHAPTER 6

The spider bite on his hand was throbbing. He tossed and turned in bed all night. It was officially the worst night's sleep of Miles Morales's life.

Miles didn't really remember much after the spider bit his hand. His uncle told them they had to leave, and somehow, they made their way back through the subway tunnels and aboveground.

How did I get back to the dorm? Miles wondered.

His hand burned. He looked down and saw the place where the spider had bitten him. In the dim light of his dorm room, Miles swore that the bite was glowing.

Spider bites do not glow, right? Man, this is not cool. . . .

He woke with a start, only to see Ganke sitting there at his computer, working, not noticing anything Miles did.

Was he awake all night? Miles thought. *Did he see me come in?*

He jumped out of bed and put on his pants.

That's weird, Miles thought. *My pants . . . shrank?*

It was true. The pants looked like high-waters–they looked like something he might have worn a couple of years ago. That's when Miles realized the pants hadn't shrunk. He had grown.

Overnight.

"I think I hit puberty," Miles said.

To Miles's complete lack of surprise, Ganke didn't respond. He didn't do anything except stop typing for just a second. Then he resumed, as if Miles hadn't said anything.

I should have kept that to myself, he thought.

A little while later Miles was walking down the school hallway, trying to silence his own inner monologue, which seemed to be getting louder by the minute.

What's going on with me?

Something weird is happening.

Why are all my thoughts so loud?!

"Are you okay?"

Miles turned to see the new girl, the one he had talked to the other day in physics class before he got in trouble.

"Huh?" Miles asked, out of it.

"Why are you so sweaty?" she asked.

Miles thought for a second, and realized that she was absolutely right—he was sweating profusely. His mind was racing, wondering if this was a side effect of that weird spider bite, and what that might mean.

Am I dying?

"It's a, uh, a puberty thing," Miles said, trying to sound like he knew what he was talking about. "I don't know why I said that. I'm not going through puberty. I mean, I am, but—"

He saw the new girl just looking at him like he had five heads.

Change tack, Miles.

"So, you're, like, new here, right? We got that in common," Miles said, trying to sound cool.

"Yeah," the girl said, agreeing with Miles, but not really. "That's one thing."

"Cool, yeah. I'm Miles."

"I'm G–*Waaaaanda*," the girl said.

"Wait, your name is Gwanda?" Miles said, genuinely interested.

Gwanda nodded. "Yes, it's African. I'm South African. No accent, though, 'cause I was raised here."

34

While they talked, Miles thought that maybe it was time to try the shoulder-touch thing that his uncle had told him about. But what if it backfired? What if she thought he was a creep?

Why is this so scary?

He took a sudden, sharp breath, and touched Gwanda's shoulder, just a little.

"I'm kidding," she said. "My name is Wanda. No *G*. That's crazy."

"Hey," Miles said, white-knuckling the moment.

"Okay then, I'll see you around," Wanda said.

"Oh, see you!" Miles said.

Wanda turned to leave, but Miles found that he couldn't let go of her shoulder.

Literally.

His fingers were stuck to her shoulder as if they had been glued in place. He tugged, but nothing happened.

"Hey, um, can you let go, please?" Wanda said, struggling to break free. Miles tried to pull his hand away, but as Wanda squirmed, her hair got in the way, and suddenly, he was stuck to that, too. "Ow, ow, ow, ow, ow! Calm down!"

"I . . . can't let go!" Miles said, pulling as hard as he could.

"Miles, let go!" Wanda said impatiently.

"I'm working on it!" Miles shot back. "It's just puberty!"

"I don't think you know what puberty is," Wanda snapped. "Just relax."

"Okay, I have a plan," Miles said.

I do have a plan, right?

"Great," Wanda said sarcastically.

"I'm going to pull really hard," Miles said.

Wanda thought for a second. "That's a terrible plan."

"One . . . two . . ."

"Don't do this," Wanda warned. When it became clear Miles was going to go through with it, she shouted, "Three!" and to Miles's shock, Wanda flipped him over with ease and slammed him onto his back with a loud *thud*.

He walked down the hallway, staring at his hair-covered hand. He couldn't believe that they had to go to the nurse, and that she had to cut Wanda's hair in order to get Miles's hand off.

Everyone's staring at me, Miles thought. *I feel like such a freak.*

He was lost in his thoughts and hardly noticed when a security guard rounded the corner.

"Hey!" the guard said, recognizing Miles. "I know you snuck out last night, Morales!"

Miles's heart jumped, and he bolted as fast as his legs would take him.

"Come back here!" the security guard yelled, and gave chase.

Miles darted ahead and raced around a corner. He opened the first door he saw, entered, and slammed the door shut behind him.

I'm safe, I'm safe, I'm safe. . . .

Then he saw whose office it was. Photos of the security guard on the wall. And a big plaque on the desk that said MARK WITTELS, SECURITY GUARD.

I'm not safe, I'm not safe, I'm not safe. . . .

Instinctively, Miles pressed his hands against the door to hold it shut just in case—

"What are you doing in my office, Morales?!"

In case of that.

The security guard was already outside the door. There was nowhere to run.

That's when Miles realized that his hands were positively glued to the door. He tried to pull them away, but it was just like with Wanda's hair. He tugged—and nothing. So he yanked even harder, and his hands came away, along with the door's plywood veneer.

He tried to wipe his hands on his shirt, knocking the veneer to the ground, but now his hands were stuck to his shirt. In a frenzy, Miles accidentally hoisted the shirt over his head, blocking his eyes. Panicked, he ran directly into a

37

bookshelf and stuck to that, too, pulling it down in front of the door, blocking it.

"Morales!" the security guard bellowed. "Open up! Open up! Security!"

"Why is this happening?" Miles said out loud.

"Hey! Open up, right now!"

Not done stumbling, Miles tripped and hit the wall, sticking to it. His momentum threw him upward, and before he could do anything to stop it, Miles found himself rolling up the wall, around the ceiling, and toward the other walls!

"Stop sticking!" Miles said to himself. "Stop . . . sticking!"

Right on cue, Miles fell from the ceiling and onto a desk chair. Then the chair started to roll, sending Miles straight for an open window.

The chair smashed into the wall, and Miles was flung free. Instinctively, he kicked out right as he went through the window, and his feet caught the windowsill. They stuck. Now Miles was standing—*horizontally*—outside the building.

He heard the security guard hammering on the door, trying to enter the office.

Not knowing what else to do, he stuck to the wall again and started to roll to an adjacent window. A class was in session inside, and the students were so transfixed by the lesson that they didn't notice the stunned face of Miles Morales staring at them, looking for help.

Unable to enter through the closed window, Miles started to roll again, taking himself on a solo tour around the exterior of the building itself. Only too late did he become aware of the flapping sound of the birds that flew right past him. Miles tried to shoo them away, but like everything else, now the birds had become affixed to his hands.

The birds started to peck at Miles's eyes, flapping their wings in a bid to escape.

Shaking his hands as fast as he could, Miles somehow managed to unstick himself from the birds. He kept rolling around the building until he finally came to a window he recognized.

His room.

He rolled right through the window and landed on his floor with a loud *thud*. He saw a pile of books around him, including some of Ganke's comics, the ones he had been reading the other night. One of them stood out in particular.

It was a Spider-Man comic, with a cover line that blared, *The True Story of Spider-Man's Origin!*

In wonderment, Miles picked up the comic, his hands sticking to it, ripping the paper just a bit. As he flipped through the pages, he saw nearly the same events that had just happened to him. Except in the comic, it wasn't Miles. It was a kid named Billy Barker. Everything was there. The spider bite. Pulling on the door, rolling out the window, hitting the floor.

"How can there be two Spider-Men?" Miles wondered. "There can't be two Spider-Men!"

"Open up!"

Miles jerked his head toward the door to his dorm room. It was the security guard.

"Hey! Open up right now!"

A second later, the door opened, and the security guard poked his head inside.

Miles wasn't there.

The guard scratched his head, muttered under his breath, then turned away and closed the door.

With a relieved Miles stuck smack to the back of it.

CHAPTER 7

"**C**ome on, Uncle Aaron! Pick up! Pick up!"

Miles paced down the Brooklyn street as the sun set, desperate to get his uncle on the phone. Maybe he would know what to do.

That's nuts, Miles thought. *What am I gonna tell him? Hey, Uncle Aaron, you know how we were out tagging subway walls last night? Well, I got bit by a glowing spider, and now I have all sorts of crazy powers and I'm taller and I sweat a lot and also I stick to stuff like hair. . . .*

"Yo, it's Aaron," came his uncle's voice, and for a second, Miles was ready to unburden himself. Until his uncle kept talking: "I'm outta town for a few days. Hit you when I'm back. Peace."

No, no, no, no, no . . .

Suddenly, Miles heard the screeching of tires on pavement. He looked up to see that he had wandered right into the middle of the street, and a car was barreling toward him. That was it. His number was up.

Except it wasn't.

Because Miles vaulted over the car and landed some twenty feet away.

What the–?!

Some kids on the street saw what happened and broke into spontaneous applause.

Freaked out, Miles raced into the subway entrance just up ahead. He looked down at his phone and briefly thought about calling his parents. But talking to his uncle was one thing. Telling his mom what was going on? Or his dad?

I don't think so.

He continued down the stairs and waited for the next train on the platform.

Miles got off the train and waited for the subway to leave the station. Then he leaped down onto the tracks and walked into the tunnel. After a while, he came to the fence that he and his uncle had jumped the previous night.

And tonight, he really jumped it. One jump and over. No climbing.

He came upon the mural that he and his uncle had been painting. Then he started his search in earnest.

Gotta be around here somewhere . . .

He combed the rubble on the ground, looking for any sign of it.

There it is!

The spider that had bitten Miles was on the ground, dead. Flipping it over, Miles saw that it was still glowing. Maybe not as bright as it had been last night, but glowing nonetheless.

"See?" Miles said aloud. "It's a normal spider. So normal. It's, like, boring how normal the spider is. . . ."

A low rumbling sound in the distance broke Miles's train of thought, and he looked up. Beyond the mural, there was an entrance to a dark, abandoned subway tunnel. The rumble grew louder, and Miles felt the vibrations in his feet.

And he felt something else.

It was like a burning . . . no, it was more like a buzzing sensation at the base of his skull. Like someone was taking an electric razor and pushing down on his neck in one spot.

Just when I thought things couldn't get any weirder . . .

Miles took a step toward the abandoned tunnel, and he felt the strange tingling at the back of his neck intensify.

"Please tell me there's a way to turn this off," he said softly, hoping someone, somewhere was listening and could do something about it.

Pressing a button on his phone, Miles activated a flashlight app to throw some light on the situation. He entered the tunnel. It was practically silent except for the sound of his own breathing.

He was breathing hard.

This is scary.

As he walked ahead, he came across a shiny metallic surface that looked like a tube. Coming closer, Miles saw there was writing on it: ALCHEMAX

The rumbling continued, and there was now a humming sound added to the mix.

The feeling at the back of his neck grew stronger. So Miles kept going.

He started to run, noticing that the farther he went, the more intense the sensation at the base of his skull became. He turned a corner, and the sensation flared to the point where Miles was sure he was going to jump out of his skin.

Jump!

Almost reflexively, Miles did jump and narrowly missed getting wrecked by a subway car that was hurtling out of the darkness through the air.

44

Miles landed safely on the ground just as the car smashed into the wall.

Oh man, oh man, oh man . . .

Miles whipped his head around to follow the car's trajectory and saw a hole in the wall beyond. Peering in, he couldn't believe his eyes.

CHAPTER 8

"**N**orm! Norm. Look at me. You're a scientist—you know how dangerous this experiment is?"

That's . . . that's Spider-Man! Miles thought. *The real Spider-Man!*

And it was. As he looked through the hole in the wall, Miles saw him, jumping and flipping around a room full of scientific equipment. But he wasn't jumping and flipping around just to get a workout. He was avoiding something.

Someone.

"Why aren't you helping me stop it?" Spider-Man said.

"It's not up to me," came a dark, threatening voice.

Miles turned and saw a twenty-five-foot-tall beastly-looking creature. It was definitely more monster than person. It had wings, and a long, gross blue tongue.

It was the Green Goblin.

Miles had seen videos on YouTube of him fighting Spider-Man before but never thought he'd see a battle like this up close.

"To whom is it up?" Spider-Man asked.

"I think I'm gonna go," Miles said quietly.

"Why, why don't you quit?!" said the Goblin, unfurling his wings.

"I could ask you the same thing. You know, I guess I like Brooklyn not being sucked into a black hole. Staten Island, maybe. Not Brooklyn!" Spider-Man quipped. "For a man with such large ears, you're a horrible listener, Norm!"

I can't believe this is happening. . . .

The Goblin threw a handful of something at Spider-Man, and the somethings exploded, knocking Spider-Man to the ground. One of the bombs rolled, unexploded, over to Miles.

"Oh, come on!" Miles cursed as he rolled away, narrowly avoiding the coming explosion. Unfortunately, he was now out in the open, an unwilling participant in a battle between Super Hero and Super Villain. Every time someone threw a piece of equipment, it jostled the ground, knocking Miles about. He tried to take cover behind some debris, but the Goblin's wings brushed it aside. Miles slid noiselessly down the floor and scrambled to gain his footing.

This is way too real.

Miles took note of his surroundings and saw that he was inside a massive chamber that contained a huge piece of equipment with tubes leading into it. He seemed to be on a platform elevated about midway through the room.

Then he heard a computerized voice say, *Initializing secondary ignition sequence.*

I like the other room better, Miles thought.

What happened next was all a blur to Miles. He saw Spider-Man and the Goblin up above him, fighting on another elevated platform. The ground rumbled. Miles slipped from his platform and fell.

Then he stopped falling.

Because Spider-Man caught him.

He swung with Miles, and they landed on a deck high above all the equipment below.

"Did you know your shoes are untied?" Spider-Man said.

Miles was speechless. He could barely say, "Uh-huh."

"This is a onesie," Spider-Man continued, "so I don't really have to worry about that."

Then Miles felt that weird buzzing at the base of his skull again.

Spider-Man looked at him, then cocked his head. Like he was recognizing something.

48

Someone.

"I thought I was the only one," Spider-Man said. "You're like me."

How does he know?

"I don't want to be," Miles said.

"I don't think you have a choice, kiddo. Got a lot going through your head, I'm sure."

"Yeah" was all a stunned Miles could manage.

Spider-Man motioned for Miles to sit tight. "You're gonna be fine. I can help you. If you stick around, I can show you the ropes," he said, trying to reassure Miles. Then Spidey turned away to face the ledge. "I just need to destroy this big machine real quick before the space-time continuum collapses. Don't move. See you in a bit!"

Jumping off the platform, Spider-Man executed a swing-flip, and suddenly he was hanging upside down from the ceiling.

He scampered across the ceiling to a panel. He tore it open, and Miles saw a slew of complicated-looking mul-ticolored wiring. Then Spidey pulled something from his suit. Miles couldn't see exactly what it was, but the wall-crawler plugged it into a port hanging from the panel.

What's he doing?

"All right, folks," Spider-Man yelled, "the party's over!"

"The party, Spider-Man, is just beginning," a deep voice said, resonating throughout the chamber. "And I don't recall inviting you."

A man stepped out of the shadows. But he wasn't just a man. He was a huge man. Massive. Built like a wall.

Miles knew who he was. Wilson Fisk. Fisk Industries.

"The party metaphor was a bad idea," Spider-Man said, looking up. "Oh boy."

Miles could do nothing as the scene unfolded. In a flash, a blur of purple moved before his eyes, striking Spider-Man. It was a man wearing a mask, with clawed gloves and heavy boots.

"Prowler, man, I was in the middle of something!" Spider-Man said in a daze. It was clear that the Prowler's blows had him shaken. "I am so tired. . . ."

The Prowler jumped right for Spider-Man, but the web-slinger recovered enough to dodge the claws and evade the kicks.

Until he couldn't, and the Prowler connected with a roundhouse kick, sending Spider-Man into the wall of the giant machinery below.

"Are you mad at me?" Spider-Man asked. "I feel like you're mad at me."

Dumbfounded, Miles could only watch. Not knowing

what else to do, he grabbed his cell phone and snapped a picture of the web-slinger in action.

"Is that all you got?" Spider-Man asked, catching his breath.

Miles peered down and saw the Goblin land on Spider-Man, pinning the hero to the ground.

"Ugh, so gross," Spider-Man groaned, jerking his head away from the Goblin's slimy tongue.

The urge to do something, to help Spider-Man–to stand and fight–came over Miles. But along with it came the fear. The fear of putting himself in mortal danger. Of what his mom–and his dad–would think. Fear.

"Spider-Man, you came all this way," Fisk said. "Watch the test. It's a hell of a freakin' light show. You're gonna love this."

"No! No!" Spider-Man yelled, his voice sounding desperate. "Don't do this! Stop! You don't know what it can do! You'll kill us all!"

From his perch, Miles watched helplessly as the machinery below came to life, roaring like some kind of raging behemoth. He swore that he heard Spider-Man shout "No!" again, but he couldn't be sure–Miles could barely hear anything over the sound of the machine.

Everything was vibrating, and Miles felt like he was

going to be thrown off the platform. He grabbed on, trying to stay flat, praying that the weird force that caused him to stick to Wanda earlier that day was in effect now.

Now there was some kind of crazy psychedelic light show going on below. Miles squinted, trying to see what was happening. He could make out only brief flashes, snapshots—

–Spider-Man struggling with the Goblin.

–Spider-Man leaping away.

–The Goblin catching Spider-Man.

–The light growing brighter. A beam, circling, spiraling, brilliant colors.

–The Goblin pulling Spider-Man into the beam.

Then a burst of color and light that nearly blinded Miles.

CHAPTER 9

*A*m *I dead?*

Miles blinked a few times. The colors started to go away, and he saw the smoke-filled chamber all around him.

No, I'm not dead. But everything hurts.

He found himself atop a pile of rubble, and realized that in the aftermath of the explosion or pulse or whatever it was, he must have been knocked off the platform and fallen to the ground below. He wasn't sure how he had survived, but he thought his newfound abilities must have had something to do with it.

Standing up, Miles saw the Green Goblin. Rather, what was left of him. The monster had been squashed beneath the remains of some heavy machinery. It wasn't pretty.

And then he saw Spider-Man.

"Hey!" Miles said, racing over to the wall-crawler. "Are you okay?!"

Miles could hear Spider-Man wheezing, and saw his body was trapped by more machinery.

"I'm fine, I'm fine," Spider-Man said, struggling to speak. "Just resting."

Miles heard a commotion from above. He looked up and saw shadows moving.

"Find him," came a voice. *Fisk.* "Now, he's here. Somewhere."

And then Miles saw them. Fisk's men.

"Listen, we gotta team up here—we don't have that much time," Spider-Man started, brandishing a small thumb drive. "This override key is the only way to stop the collider. Up top, just swing-flip, crawl to the panel, pop it in. Red button, 'kay?"

"I can't do anything," Miles protested. "I'm only thirteen!"

"Thirteen?" Spider-Man said, considering it. "Aw, man. That's young."

"Can you get up?" Miles asked.

"Yeah, yeah, I always get up." Spider-Man tried to laugh, but a deep, wet cough came out instead. "The coughing's probably not a good sign," he managed. "Listen," he added quickly. "You need a mask. You need to hide your face. You don't tell anyone who you are. No one can know. He's got everyone in his pocket."

"What?" Miles said.

This is all happening too fast. . . .

"If he turns the machine on again, everything you know will disappear! Your family—everyone! Everyone. Promise me you'll do this."

Miles swallowed hard. "I promise."

"Go!" Spider-Man shouted, his voice sounding weaker than before. "Destroy the collider. I'll come find you. . . . It's going to be okay."

Miles heard them coming closer, Fisk's men. He took the thumb drive from Spider-Man, and then he scrambled over a pile of debris.

From his vantage point, Miles saw the men arrive, Fisk right behind them. Fisk towered over Spider-Man, gloating.

"We're done with the tests. I want what I've been promised. Two days," Fisk said, talking to someone Miles couldn't see. Then Fisk turned to Spider-Man. "I'd say it's nice to see you again, Spider-Man. But it isn't."

"Hey, Kingpin," Spider-Man said, struggling to breathe. "How's business?"

"Booming."

"Nice," Spider-Man answered.

Then the massive man reached down with a meaty hand, grabbed Spider-Man's mask, and yanked it off.

Miles squinted. It was a guy with blond hair. Older than Miles, for sure. Maybe in his twenties.

"You look different than I expected," Fisk joked.

"You mean more handsome?" Spider-Man replied, wheezing.

"Prowler," Fisk replied. "Do the honors."

Miles saw the purple-clad figure of the Prowler emerge from darkness below, raising his claws and moving toward Spider-Man.

"Don't you want to know what I saw in there?" Spider-Man said, his voice frantic.

"Wait!" Fisk ordered, raising his hand. The Prowler stopped in his tracks.

"This might open a black hole under Brooklyn," Spider-Man said. "You own Brooklyn—why would you do that?"

"It's not always about the money, Spider-Man," Fisk said with a frown.

"I know what you're trying to do," Spider-Man said. "It won't work. They're gone."

Fisk glared at Spider-Man and reached out with his hands. Miles could only watch as the giant man ended the life of the city's webbed protector.

Then Miles screamed.

Fisk's eyes shot upward, and Miles knew that he had been noticed.

"Kill that kid" was all Miles heard as he saw the Prowler leap his way.

CHAPTER 10

Miles felt as if his whole body was on autopilot. He was running, legs pumping, through the dark tunnel that had led him to Spider-Man in the first place.

He came to the fence, hopped it in one leap, didn't even have to think about it.

Heavy footsteps followed right behind, catching up, closer, closer.

The Prowler.

Miles hit the ground and started to run.

The Prowler was nearly on top of him.

Miles could practically feel the Prowler's claws on his back.

The weird feeling at the base of his skull returned, and Miles turned to see that a subway train was barreling down the tunnel, heading right for him. He jumped into the air, hands and feet hitting the ceiling, and the train thundered beneath him.

He clung tightly to the top of the tunnel as stale air rushed all around him.

The train passed, and Miles saw the Prowler waiting for him. Now he was walking—as if like he knew that his prey wasn't going anywhere. Miles yanked his hands to disengage from the ceiling.

They were stuck.

Not again! No, no, no, not now!

The Prowler only feet away.

Miles yanking his hands.

Nothing.

Miles pulling harder than he had before.

A ripping sound.

The skin on his hands tearing.

Miles hitting the ground.

The boy ran. He heard the sound of another train coming and sprinted for the platform, maybe twenty feet away. The train was rolling into the station. Miles had one chance at this. He ran, the Prowler right behind him. Then Miles jumped.

He hit the platform, and the train pulled in. The Prowler

was on the other side of the train. Miles had bought himself a few seconds.

He leaped up the stairs to the street above.

Miles had made it.

Welcome to the Spider-Verse!

A 13-year-old Brooklyn native, Miles is a Spider-Man unlike any we've seen before. He's a bright teenager who likes hanging out with friends and being a kid. But what his friends don't know is that Miles is also learning to embrace an entirely new and unexpected life as the all-new Spider-Man!

JEFFERSON DAVIS

Miles's dad, a dedicated police officer, is always trying to steer his son down the right path and push him to live up to his full potential. Miles and Jefferson may clash when it comes to what that potential looks like, but beneath the surface there's a whole lot of love between them.

RIO MORALES

Miles's mother, a nurse, loves her baby boy to pieces and is always trying to protect him from the harsh realities of the world. Not an easy thing to do when your teenager secretly doubles as Spider-Man!

GANKE

As roommates at Brooklyn Visions Academy, Miles and Ganke have overcome a rocky start and become close friends, bonding over their mutual love of Spider-Man comics.

UNCLE AARON

Jefferson's estranged brother, Uncle Aaron is a friend and mentor to Miles when he needs one the most, encouraging Miles to be true to himself and follow his passions.

PETER PARKER

Years of Super Hero life have taken a toll on Peter Parker. Peter never thought that he'd end up being a mentor to a younger generation of heroes, but training Miles Morales, an all-new Spider-Man, to understand the importance of power and responsibility has given Peter a new positive outlook on life.

SPIDER-GWEN

Spunky and free-spirited Gwen Stacy, 15, is her world's Spider-Woman and known as Spider-Gwen! Intelligent and quick-witted, Gwen has a sharp sense of humor and is a natural leader. After getting pulled from her world and thrown into Miles's, she is deperate to get home, but she also finds time to help Miles adjust to his new powers.

SPIDER-MAN NOIR

A Peter Parker from a parallel universe, this Spidey is a darker, more serious version of Spider-Man who fought crime during the Great Depression in 1933. Unlike most Spider-People, Spider-Man Noir doesn't have much of a sense of humor. He *does* have an old-fashioned perspective that makes it harder for him to adjust to Miles's modern world.

SPIDER-HAM

It's Spider-Man . . . as a cartoon pig! Spider-Ham, aka Peter Porker, is a sweet, well-intentioned member of the Spider Family. He is always one to try to pay a compliment or crack a joke, but despite behaving like the ultimate ham, he takes his job as Spider-Man seriously and fights alongside the others with his special kind of cartoon fury.

PENI PARKER & SP//dr

A 13-year-old girl from a futuristic New York, Peni is an expressive, tantrum-prone vigilante who doesn't wear the typical Spider-Man suit. Instead, she has a super high-tech robotic Spidey suit that responds to only her DNA.

CHAPTER 11

"Why aren't you at school?"

Miles had tried to be so quiet as he climbed up the wall and jumped into his bedroom through the window. But he should have known that his dad would hear. The moment Miles saw his dad, he ran up to him and hugged him tight.

Jefferson didn't seem to know how to react at first. Then he embraced his son, hugging him close. "Whoa, whoa," he said, trying to soothe Miles. "It's okay."

"Miles? ¿Qué te pasa?" his mom said, entering Miles's bedroom. She was surprised to see her son at home, too. "Is it the earthquake?"

Earthquake? Miles thought. *Whatever happened in that subway tunnel tonight must have been felt all over New York City!*

"Can I sleep here tonight?" Miles pleaded.

"Miles, it's a weeknight," Jefferson began. "You made a commitment to that school—"

"Jeff, he's upset."

A moment of silence as Miles's dad looked at his mom.

"Of course you can stay," Jefferson said, leaving the room.

"Dad?"

"Yeah?" Jefferson said, looking at his son.

"Do you really hate Spider-Man?" Miles asked. He had to know.

Jefferson looked at Miles, confused. "Yeah? I mean, with a vigilante there's no due—"

Then Rio shoved Jefferson out of the room. "Jeff, mi amor," she said.

"What?" Jefferson said defensively. "He asked me. Baby, you know how I feel about Spider-Man, c'mon. . . ."

As Jefferson walked down the hall, Miles settled back on his bed. Rio stroked his forehead. "Tu sabes que el te quiere mucho. . . . You know that, right?" she said tenderly. "He just wants you to have more options than he did."

Then Rio kissed Miles on the forehead, turned out the lights, and closed the door.

Miles felt like he was in a daze. Everything that happened the night before seemed like some twisted, horrible dream. Only it wasn't a dream. He had the USB drive in his pocket to remind him of that.

He stood quietly in his home. Miles saw his dad sitting on the couch, watching TV. The reports were now coming in about last night's events.

The events that Miles had witnessed firsthand.

"This is breaking news," came the voice of a reporter on the TV. "We are hearing reports that a man wearing the mask of Spider-Man was found dead in front of the *Daily Bugle* from an apparent neck injury. We can now confirm that the man's name is Peter Parker, a twenty-seven-year-old grad student.

"He was many things," the reporter continued. "Hero, guardian . . . But today, New York's scrappy champion is gone. While it may seem impossible, multiple sources confirm Peter Parker was indeed Spider-Man, leaving a permanent void in our beleaguered city."

Miles's eyes were glued to the TV as the scene cut away to interviews with various city goers. "I saw him by the bus once," one person said. "He was always saving everybody. He was still a regular guy. A good guy. Spider-Man is dead."

The reporter flashed back on-screen. "A longtime resident of Queens, Parker is survived by his wife, Mary Jane, and his aunt, May Parker."

"I'm going to miss him."

Miles turned around to see the shopkeeper right behind him. He was standing in a costume shop, not quite sure what he was doing there. In front of him were several Spider-Man costumes of varying sizes.

"Yeah," Miles replied.

"We were friends, you know," the shopkeeper said wistfully.

"Can I return it if it doesn't fit?" Miles asked, gesturing to the costume in his hands.

"It always fits," the store owner replied. "Eventually."

CHAPTER 12

I wonder when eventually will get here. This thing doesn't fit right at all!

Miles had put on the baggy costume, which bunched in all the wrong places. He wondered what he was doing. He had his own amazing set of spider-powers, and now he was dressed in the suit of the dead hero.

He was standing in a cathedral in New York City, among a sea of people also dressed like Spider-Man. Some of them were wearing full costumes, like him. Others wore home-made costumes or T-shirts and caps. All emblazoned with the familiar red-and-blue colors, the webbing, the distinctive spider eyes.

It was Peter Parker's funeral.

Miles watched as a tall woman with red hair stood at

the front of the cathedral, speaking into a microphone.

"My husband, Peter Parker, was an ordinary person. He always said it could have been anyone behind the mask, he was just the kid who happened to get bit. He didn't really know what to do or how to do it. He wasn't sure he even deserved to do it. He didn't ask for his powers, but he chose to be Spider-Man."

The woman dabbed her eyes with a handkerchief. "The things that Peter was fighting for didn't die with him. And the things he was fighting against didn't, either. If you take one thing from his example, I hope it's this: You are powerful, and we are counting on you."

The woman turned away from the dais as an older, gray-haired woman comforted her. Then Miles felt that buzzing sensation at the base of his neck once again, the hairs on his arm standing on end. He whipped his head around. He glanced outside and thought he saw something on a rooftop, something fast and fleeting.

Was that the Prowler?

Miles left the funeral, pushing his way through the thick crowd. He no longer felt the buzzing sensation, but it unnerved him nonetheless. He wasn't sure what to make of it, and he couldn't shake the feeling that the Prowler had been there.

66

Did he follow me? Miles wondered. *Does he . . . does he know who I am?*

He rounded a corner and removed something from his jacket. It was the Spider-Man comic book he had looked at in his dorm room, the one with the wall-crawler's origin story. Miles didn't know why he had taken the comic with him.

Opening it up, Miles flipped through its pages and saw panels where Spider-Man tested his newfound powers by jumping from a building.

Swallowing hard, Miles rolled up the comic, stuck it back in his jacket, and ran.

It's time to test out these new powers of mine.

Miles wasn't sure what building he ran into. He just knew that he had gone inside, opened the stairway door, and run up.

Up, up, up.

All the way up to the top floor. He didn't even feel winded. His breathing was totally normal.

Opening the door, he exited onto the rooftop. Walking to the edge, determined, Miles looked down. He was high up. High enough that he could look down and see rooftops of other buildings.

His eyes caught one rooftop, and Miles thought, *I can make that.*

Cracking his neck, Miles waited there for a moment. He took a breath, then another. Then another. Then he ran toward the edge.

And tripped on his untied shoelace.

And dropped the thumb drive—the override key—that Spider-Man had entrusted him with.

Miles landed on the key and heard a loud *CRACK*.

When Miles looked down, he saw that the key lay in pieces.

CHAPTER 13

It was cold outside.

Cold and snowing.

And Miles stood there, watching the snow fall, standing in the grounds outside the cathedral, standing at the grave of a man he barely knew.

"I'm sorry, Mr. Parker," Miles said. He held the Spider-Man mask in one hand, still wearing the costume from earlier that day. The funeral was long over, and the cathedral had emptied. Miles had hung around, waiting for everyone to leave.

"That thing you gave me, that key . . ." Miles held the USB drive in his hand. "I think I really messed it up. I want to do what you asked. I really do, but . . . I'm sorry, I can't do this without you."

"Hey! Kid!"

Miles quickly pulled the mask over his head and whirled around. He saw someone standing in the dark, moving his way. Not knowing what to do, Miles threw up his arms. There was a flash of electricity or who-knows-what from Miles's hands, and it struck the figure in front of him.

What the–?!

Then suddenly, something stringy and sticky flew from the figure in front of him, covering Miles's hands.

"No!" Miles yelled. "No way. Who are you?"

Moving forward, Miles approached the person who had been lurking but was now slumped in the shadows. He felt a flash of something at the base of his skull. Then he moved closer. Closer. Miles looked at their face. The hair was brown, but there was no mistaking the face.

It was Peter Parker.

CHAPTER 14

Miles stared at the man who looked like Peter Parker. Miles had somehow managed to bring him back to his uncle Aaron's apartment. With his uncle out of the city for a few days, it would be a perfect place to lay low and figure out exactly what was going on.

Finally, the man started to come to.

"You're like me," the man said.

"We'll see about that," Miles said, trying to sound tough.

The man glanced at his restraints and smirked. "Well, *this* is cute." He took a breath and flexed, as if to break free.

Miles gasped, took a step back, and was surprised that the ropes actually held. He had spent the last fifteen minutes tying the man to a chair, using anything he could find. Ropes, computer cables, extension cords, string—

literally, whatever he could find that could be used to bind someone.

"Okay," the man said. "Now it's less cute."

"Why do you look like Peter Parker?" Miles asked.

"Because I *am* Peter Parker."

"Then why aren't you dead?" Miles said, trying to wrap his head around the situation. "Why is your hair different? Why are you older? Why–"

"You don't look so hot, either, kid," Peter said. "Most Super Heroes don't wear their own merch." He nodded at Miles's store-bought costume.

"Are you a ghost?" Miles asked, dead serious.

Please don't be a ghost.

"No," Peter replied.

"Are you a zombie?"

Please don't be a zombie.

"Stop it."

"Am *I* a zombie?"

"You're not even close," Peter said.

Miles thought for a moment. Then he had it. "Are you from another dimension? Like, a parallel universe where things are like this universe but different? And you're Spider-Man in that universe? But somehow traveled to this universe? But you don't know how?"

"Wow," Peter said, impressed. "That was really just a guess?"

"Well, we learned about it in physics–"

"Quantum theory," Peter said, finishing Miles's thought for him.

"This is amazing!" Miles said. "You can teach me! Just like Peter said he would!"

"Before he died," Peter added.

"Yeah, exactly!"

"Yeah, all right," Peter said sarcastically.

"I made a promise to him, man," Miles said, his voice serious.

"You want to learn to be Spider-Man?"

Miles shook his head. "No, I *have* to learn to be Spider-Man."

The two Spider-Men looked at each other.

"So here's lesson number one, kid: Don't watch the mouth. Watch the hands."

Then he showed his hands to Miles. The hands that had just finished untying the binds that confined him to the chair. Miles's jaw hit the floor as Peter stood up.

The next thing Miles knew, Peter leaped in the air, kicked the chair toward Miles, and knocked him over. Then he spun a web, covering Miles's mouth so he couldn't yell.

One leap later, Peter was at the open window of Uncle Aaron's apartment.

"I'll take it from here, kid. Have a nice life, don't be a fool, stay in school," Peter said.

Don't go, don't go, don't go! Miles thought.

Peter paused in the window, turning. "Trust me, kid, this'll all make you a better Spider-Man."

Then Peter jumped right from the window.

Barely a second later, Miles heard a scream, and the sound of Peter hitting the fire escape.

"Hey, are you okay?" Miles asked, helping Peter sit up. He had tumbled down several flights of stairs and had come to rest on a fire escape a few floors down.

"No, I'm not. I don't think my atoms are real jazzed about being in the wrong dimension," Peter said. He looked at Miles. "I got a lot of stuff I've gotta deal with back home. I'm not looking for a side gig as a Spider-Man coach."

"I read the comics," Miles said. "'With great power comes great—'"

"Don't you dare finish that sentence!" Peter interrupted. "I'm sick of it! Trust me, you do not want to be Spider-Man, kid."

A weird look suddenly came over Peter's face, and his

whole body twitched, vibrating. It was as if he were out of sync or something.

What was that? Miles wondered.

"I don't have a choice," Miles protested. "Fisk has a supercollider. He's trying to kill me."

"Wait a second. What did you say?" Peter said, stopping Miles in his tracks.

"Fisk's trying to kill me!"

"Who cares about that? Where's the collider?" Peter asked.

Man, this Peter Parker sure isn't like the other Peter Parker. . . .

"Brooklyn. Under Fisk Tower."

"Good-bye!" Peter hollered as he started to run.

CHAPTER 15

"**W**here are you going?" shouted
Miles.

What is happening? he thought. *I can't even.*

As soon as Miles had mentioned the supercollider and its
maybe-it's-in-this-general-area location, Peter Parker was
off. He just flat left Miles standing on the fire escape outside
Uncle Aaron's apartment.

So Miles did the only thing he could think of.

He followed Peter.

Peter was walking up ahead and didn't seem to hear
Miles. Miles was keeping pace, walking as fast as he could,
but he was still new to this.

Not to walking—he knew how to do that.

Walking on walls. That was new.

Miles was about fifteen feet behind Peter as they walked sideways along the wall of a ten-story building. Peter got to the edge, looked around, then started to walk down the wall, toward the street. Miles was right behind him.

"When they run it again," Peter said, "I'll jump back in the—"

"You can't let them run it!" Miles said. "I'm supposed to blow it up so it never runs again, or everyone's gonna die!"

"'Or everyone is going to die,'" Peter said, and Miles could have sworn his tone was mocking. "That's what they always say. But there's always a little bit of time before everybody dies, and that's when I do my best work."

"Aren't you going to need this?" Miles said as he removed the broken override key from his pocket.

"You have a goober? Give it," Peter said, reaching out. Miles pulled back.

"Wait, no. Not so fast. He—the other Peter—called it an override key."

Peter rolled his eyes. "There's always a bypass key, a virus key, a who-cares key," he said. "I can never remember, so I always call it a goober. Give it."

"What does it do?" Miles asked.

"I'll tell you later," Peter said. "Just give it to me."

Fool me once, Miles thought. Then he shoved the override key into his mouth.

"No!" he said, mouth full of plastic and metal. "I'll swallow it—don't play with me!"

"I'm going to use it to hack the system, I'm going to tell it where to send me, jump into the portal, and I'm on my way home. Got it?"

Then Peter turned around and started to walk again.

"But I need the goober," Miles said.

What happened next, Miles wasn't completely sure. Near as he could figure, while he was talking, Peter had spun a web directly at his mouth, snagging the override key and yanking it right from his maw.

"Hey! Wait! Hey!" Miles shouted.

Peter examined the key in his hands. "Did you break this?" he asked.

"No," Miles lied quickly. "It broke. I don't remember what happened."

"This is why I never had kids. This is why I never did that."

Miles looked at the broken device, then back at Peter. "Can't we make another one?"

"We can't do anything," Peter said, sounding exasperated. "Thanks to you, I have to re-steal what your guy stole from Alchemax and make another one of these."

"The other Peter," Miles said. "He said if I don't destroy

the collider, it could rupture the space-time continuum." He paused. "Sounds like that could mess up your universe, too. Look, if you don't help me, you won't have a home to go home to."

"Well, this sucks," Peter said moodily. "Come on, kid, we have a very important first stop!"

Miles smiled.

Victory.

Miles couldn't believe that this was the "very important first stop." He sat across the table from Peter Parker and watched as he shoved a massive burger dripping with every condiment known to man into his mouth.

"I love this burger," Peter said, mouth full of food. "So delicious. One of the best burgers I've ever had. In my universe, this place closed six years ago. I don't know why. I really don't."

Miles rolled his eyes. The fate of the world was at stake, and here he was, sitting in a diner, watching the Spider-Man from another universe eating a burger.

"Can we focus?" Miles begged.

In response, Peter dumped a load of fries from a greasy bag onto the table. Then he spread them out with his hands and picked up a single, soggy stick of potato.

"Okay," Peter said, sounding like a teacher. "This fry

is your universe. It's soggy, it's undercooked, it's small, it's weird, it's gross—it wants to grow up to be a better universe."

Miles sighed.

Then Peter pointed at another french fry. "And this crispy, delicious, normal fry is my universe."

"So how'd that bring you here?" Miles asked.

"Quantum entanglement," Peter answered. "Spider-Man from your universe is another version of me. His quantum signature sucked me here through some portal made by Fisk's collider."

Miles scratched his head. "What does Fisk want with a portal to different dimensions?"

Peter shrugged. "I don't know. He's your Fisk, not mine. And I need to use that portal to get me from your french fry to my french fry. I call it *Spider-Man: Home-going.*"

Pointing at the pile of fries, Miles said, "There's a version of you in every one of these?"

Peter shrugged again. "I hope not."

"The other Peter—"

"If you don't mind, let's call him Dead Peter, just to avoid the confusion."

Miles's eyes went wide. "Uh, no? The other Peter said he was going to be showing me the ropes. You got any Spider-Man tips you can tell me now?"

"Yeah, I got plenty," Peter said, chewing. "Disinfect the mask. You're gonna want to use baby powder in the suit, heavy on the joints. You can't have any chafing, right?"

"Anything else?" Miles asked in disbelief.

"Nope, that was everything."

"I think you're gonna be a bad teacher," Miles said.

"We'll see. Look up where Alchemax is."

Whipping out his phone, Miles did a quick search and started reading. "'Alchemax is a private technological campus in Hudson Valley, New York.'"

Peter slapped the table, causing the pile of fries to scatter. "Well, there you go. We're going to Hudson Valley."

"Good," Miles said, anxious to start. "You can teach me to swing on the way there."

Peter laughed.

CHAPTER 16

The bus ride from Manhattan to New York's Hudson Valley took almost three hours. At first, Miles thought maybe they could web-swing their way to Alchemax, but Peter was a little more practical about their situation.

The bus let them off about a mile away from the Alchemax facility. From there, they walked. They started on the road, but as they got closer, Miles and Peter entered the woods that lined the street. Where they were going, they might just need the element of surprise.

Miles saw the labs from a distance. Star looking buildings dotted the landscape. He saw a bunch of big, brutish guys walking around outside.

"So how do we retrace Peter's steps?" Miles asked.

"That's a good question," Peter said. "What would I do if I were me?"

Huh? Oh, right.

"Okay, got it. Step one: I infiltrate the lab," Peter started. "Two: find the head scientist's computer. Step three: I hack the computer—"

"It's not technically hacking," Miles corrected. "It's kinda—"

"Not now, hold on. I just lost my train of thought. Step four: download the important stuff. I'll know it when I see it. And step five: I grab a bagel from the cafeteria and run."

Peter finished going through the steps, none of which seemed to include Miles.

"So what am I doing?" Miles asked.

"Step six: You stay here. You're lookout," Peter replied. "Very important."

Frustrated, Miles was near his breaking point. "Look, man, you have to teach me to do Spider-Man stuff or I'm not going to be able to help—"

"All right!" Peter said. "Watch and learn, kid. I'll quiz you later. You are doing great, Miles." He spun a web that hit the building, and swung away. Miles saw him reach the facility, then pry open a grate on the ground and jump inside.

Ugh. I got the worst Spider-Man.

Miles sat on the rock in the woods, alone, wondering why

he had even bothered coming out here in the first place. It wasn't like he was helping. And he wasn't learning how to use his new powers.

Oh, and he was missing school, too. Which meant there would be a phone call home to his parents to find out where Miles was.

Which means I am capital-D dead.

He wasn't sure how much time had passed when he saw the limousine pull up to the front gate. Something about the car caught his attention. Then he realized what it was– the buzzing at the base of his skull was back.

The limousine drove past the gate and up to the front entrance of the Alchemax facility. Miles gasped as he saw Wilson Fisk exit. He was flanked by a big bruiser type. The bruiser had bone-white skin, and Miles recognized him from the news as a guy called Tombstone.

No! No, no, no, no, no! Miles thought. *I should warn Peter. No, he didn't want my help. But Fisk did kill the other Spider-Man . . . and I just watched. What do I do? What do I do?*

Before he knew it, Miles had darted from the woods and into the clearing that lay between him and Alchemax. He kept low to the ground, doing his best to avoid detection.

What am I doing?

He reached the building, jumped, and disappeared

down the same grate that Peter had used to enter the facility.

Miles moved along the inside of the air vent, crawling as if it was second nature to him. Every few feet or so, he'd pass over a grate and could see what was happening in the hallway down below. He could see Fisk, and Tombstone was by his side. There were people wearing lab coats just ahead of them. Alchemax employees, Miles assumed.

I wonder what they're d–

Before he could finish his thought, Miles collided with something big.

"What are you doing here?"

Oh man, it's Peter!

"Fisk is here!" Miles whispered. "Just move over!"

"C'mon, you're stepping on my foot!" Peter complained. "Go back outside!"

"Move a little to your right . . ." Miles insisted. "I can't just sit here and let Spider-Man die without doing anything about it," he said, his voice stubborn and strong. "I'm not doing that again."

Peter looked at Miles, and his expression softened. "Most people I meet in the workplace try to kill me, so you're a nice change of pace," he said.

Down below, they watched as a woman wearing a lab

coat walked over to Fisk. Miles listened, trying to take in their conversation.

"Look at this data," the woman said. "I know you can't really understand this, but these are really good numbers. . . ."

Both Miles and Peter watched as the two continued to speak. The woman sat down at a computer and started to type, and Miles realized that Fisk and the woman weren't in a hallway anymore but a room of some kind.

Miles noticed Peter break out in a smile. "And . . . I got the password!" Peter said. "You see how cool that was?"

He watched her enter the password! How come I didn't notice that?

Miles strained to look at the scientist below. "You see this?" the woman said. She was showing something to Fisk, but Miles couldn't see what it was. "And this? This is multiple dimensions beginning to crash into each other. If we fire again this week, there could be a black hole under New York. A rupture in the space-time continuum. And that's just impractical."

Miles listened, horrified. Peter must have noticed the expression on his face, because his next words were "These are pretty standard Spider-Man stakes. You get used to it. Watch this, he's going to say, *You've got twenty-four hours!*"

Sure enough, Fisk gave a little shrug and said, "You've got twenty-four hours. No excuses!"

Maybe Peter does know what he's talking about. . . .

"Hold on, hold on," the scientist said, "Let's talk more about this—let me show you some more data. . . ."

With that, the group left the room. Peter turned to Miles. "Boom! It's go time."

"Go time?" Miles echoed. "Man, that's corny."

"Yeah, but I've always wanted to say *go time*, and I've never had anyone to say it to, so *boom!* It's go time!"

Miles wasn't reassured.

A few seconds later, Peter had clambered out of the vent and into the room below. He went right to the computer and entered the scientist's password.

"Miles," he whispered as he typed, "watch the door for—"

When Peter didn't see Miles by the door or anywhere else in the room, he looked back up at the vent. There was Miles, still trying to get out, his hands stuck.

"What are you doing?" Peter asked.

"I can't move," Miles said.

"Okay, relax your fingers," Peter advised. "Just let go, be in the moment!"

"I *am* in the moment!" Miles snapped. "It's a terrible moment!"

87

"Slow down your breathing, okay?"

Miles felt like he was going to hyperventilate. "This isn't your yoga class, man!"

"What do you do to relax?"

"Not this!" Miles barked.

"Hey! Calm down," Peter said, striking a soothing tone. "Relax, relax, calm down, calm down. . . ."

Miles took a deep breath and thought for a second. And then he started to hum to himself, quietly. He was surprised to find that he could lift one finger from the vent. Then another. In no time, he had pulled his hands free.

That was the good part of Peter's advice.

The bad part? Miles came unstuck quickly, and he fell to the ground, metal grate and all, with a resounding clang.

"Teenagers are the worst," Peter said. Suddenly, Peter leaped up from his seat as if his Spider sense had started to buzz, and went to the door. He looked through the small window.

Peter turned and glanced around for Miles. "Miles! Where'd you go? The scientist is heading back. We're making too much noise."

"I'm right here!" Miles said.

Peter had obviously heard Miles speak, but he kept looking around as if Miles weren't in the room. "Where? I can't see you!"

"I'm right in front of you," Miles said, as if he were talking to a five-year-old. "Can Spider-Man turn invisible?"

"Not in my universe," Peter said, gaping. He extended a finger outward to see if it was true.

"Ow! You just poked me in the eye!" Miles moaned.

"This is incredible!" Peter said. "Some kind of fight-or-flight thing."

But they didn't have time to ponder this amazing discovery. The sound of footsteps grew closer. Peter turned to the invisible Miles and said, "Stay invisible and download the schematics!" Then he gave Miles the password to the computer.

How do I do this? I don't know how to . . . What is Peter thinking?!

The door opened, and the scientist was clearly stunned to find Spider-Man standing in the middle of the room.

"Spider-Man?"

"Oh, hey!" Peter said to the scientist. "Didn't see you there."

"Well, this is kinda trippy," the scientist said, clearly puzzled. "You're supposed to be dead."

"Surprise!" Spider-Man joked.

He wasn't ready for what came next. The scientist grabbed the edge of Peter's mask, and before he could stop her, she ripped it off. "This is fascinating," she said, looking at Peter. "An entirely different Peter Parker."

While Peter dealt with the scientist, Miles quietly made his way to the computer. He sat down and typed in the password, hoping he had remembered the combination of letters and numbers correctly.

"Okay, that's m'face," Peter said as the scientist started to pull at his cheeks.

Miles sat at the computer, barely paying attention to Peter and the scientist. He was intent on getting the files he needed from the computer. Once he got in, though, he had no idea what to take. So he decided to take all the files. He dumped them into a folder, and then started to copy every-thing over.

Which is when the computer suddenly froze.

Not knowing what else to do, Miles unplugged the com-puter, and tucked it in his arms, monitor and all. He looked over at Peter, who stared at him. Rather, Miles assumed he was staring at him, but in reality, Peter was watching the computer "float" through the air, due to Miles's invisibility.

"And obviously, you've been glitching," the woman said to Peter.

Glitching? Miles thought. *Just like he did outside Uncle Aaron's apartment.*

90

"Glitching?" Peter said, playing it cool. "No. Why would you even say that?"

"If you stay in this dimension too long, your body's going to disintegrate," the scientist said. And then the tone of her voice took a creepy turn. "It's going to be very painful and very interesting. I think I'll watch."

Then she moved her wrist toward her mouth and spoke into her watch. "Get Fisk. Tell him I've got proof."

"What did you say your name was?" Peter said, slowly walking toward the door.

The woman smiled at Peter, but it was anything but friendly. "Oh, I didn't. My name is Dr. Olivia Octavius. I was bummed I didn't get to see you die the first time."

"Can I assume your friends call you Doc Ock?" Peter asked.

"My *friends* call me Liv," she said. "My *enemies* call me Doc Ock."

Moving at blinding speed, Peter spun a web to a panel that controlled the door and opened it.

"I got this!" he shouted to Miles. "Run!"

CHAPTER 17

Miles was running down the hall, fumbling with the computer and monitor. They weren't heavy, not with his spider-strength. But they were clumsy and awkward, and not exactly ideal things to be trying to run with.

As he ran, he noticed something peculiar. One moment, he was invisible, and the next, completely visible. He was like a human strobe light, flashing on and off.

He was so focused on his predicament that he didn't even see the lab assistant until after he plowed right into her. They both landed on the floor.

"Dah!" Miles shouted. "Sorry!"

"*Dah!*" the lab assistant shouted back.

"I'm so sorry. Gotta go!"

With that, Miles got up and started to run, but not before noting that the lab assistant looked oddly familiar.

Kind of like Wanda . . .

The next thing Miles knew, Peter smashed through the wall in front of him, landing at Miles's feet amid the rubble. He saw a flash of something metallic through the hole from which Peter had burst.

Miles stood there, invisible yet again and dumbfounded. He held up the computer and monitor and shrugged.

"All right, let me tell you the good news. We don't need the monitor," Peter said. He grabbed it from Miles and threw it down. Then he spun a web and was already swinging through the door when Miles saw it.

Well, her.

It was the scientist, the one from before. Except she looked . . . different. She was sporting a harness of some kind, with four metallic arms that held her aloft. She towered over Miles.

"Peter, you didn't tell me you had an invisible friend," Doc Ock said, menace tainting her every word.

"Peter!" Miles screamed.

"Can you give that back, young man? It's proprietary."

Doc Ock stepped through the hole in the wall. The

tentacles that whipped around her threatened to crush Miles if he so much as moved.

So he didn't.

But the tentacles did.

One snaked its way toward Miles, moving as if it were alive. Miles gasped when Peter suddenly yanked him through the door.

Miles was panting beneath his mask, holding on to the computer for dear life. It took him a second to realize that he wasn't in immediate danger. He and Peter were still in the Alchemax facility, but they were now in a large, fairly crowded room. There were people sitting at tables, all staring at the two weirdos wearing Halloween costumes. On one side of the room, there was a long display case filled with food.

The cafeteria.

"This'd be a good time to turn invisible," Peter said softly, without looking at Miles.

"Yup," Miles agreed.

"Spider-Man?" asked one of the security guards in the room, walking closer.

"You know, it's funny—I get that a lot," Peter said.

"Hey," Miles added.

Then the security guard pulled a weapon, and suddenly the other people sitting stood up and followed suit.

"Hey!" one of them shouted. "Hands up!"

Peter and Miles sprinted from the cafeteria and ran through the doors. They were now outside, and Miles could see the forest in the distance.

"Time to swing," Peter said, "just like I taught you!"

"When did you teach me that?" Miles said.

"I didn't. It's a little joke for team-building!" Peter replied, then he tossed one of his web shooters to Miles. "Let's go!"

What am I supposed to do with this? he thought. *I don't know what to do with th–*

Then Peter pushed him off the roof.

"Hurry up!"

Peter was up ahead, but Miles was just not getting the hang of it. He was trying to shoot the web shooter straight, but he kept getting all twisted. It didn't help that the security guards on the ground below were shooting at them.

This is nuts, Miles thought. *I gotta get out of the trees before they shoot me down.*

Miles let go of the web and dropped to the forest floor below. Then he started to run.

"What are you doing down there?" Peter yelled at him.

"I run better than I swing!" Miles said, legs pumping.

"You gotta swing or they'll catch you!"

Miles reached the end of his rope. "Well, maybe you shoulda taught me, instead of eating that cheeseburger!"

Without warning, Miles felt the buzzing at the base of his skull that he had come to realize meant danger was near. A moment later, he heard a metallic buzzing sound, and then saw Doc Ock cutting down trees with a buzz-saw tentacle, coming closer.

Realizing that Peter was right, Miles aimed his web shooter at a tree branch and pressed the trigger on his palm.

THWIP!

A miss.

"Aim with your hips!" Miles whipped his head around and saw Peter doubling back after him. "Look where you want it to hit. Square your shoulders! Don't forget to follow through. Don't shoot off your back foot!"

The sound of the buzz saw grew closer, and in desperation, Miles ran straight up a tree.

"That's too many things!" Miles shouted.

"Then stop listening to me!"

"What kind of teacher are you?"

As Doc Ock neared, Miles aimed his web shooter

at a distant tree and squared his shoulders. Then, once again, he pressed the palm trigger.

THWIP!

The web snagged the exact branch Miles had been staring at.

"Oh, thank you!" Miles called out. "Woo! I'm doing it!"

"That's really good, Miles!" Peter said, watching Miles swing to the next tree. "That was really good! You actually listened to everything I said."

"Okay," Miles said, somehow feeling that Peter was taking credit for Miles's success.

"Look at us," Peter added. "We're a little team. Me as the teacher who can still do it, you as the student who can do it, just not as good. I'm proud of us! Is there something you want to say to me?"

But before Miles could say anything, Peter flickered, glitching, and fell from the tree onto a branch below.

Instinctively, Miles launched himself toward Peter. He landed right next to him, but the impact caused the branch to break, sending him and Peter to the ground. Along with the computer that Miles had been carrying.

The computer fell right into Doc Ock's waiting arms.

Doc Ock smiled. She had what she wanted. Between her and the security guards, they would take care of Miles and Peter.

I can't believe this is how it ends.

And the next thing Miles knew, a blur of black, white, and pink swung by, plowing right into Doc Ock. Miles once again had possession of the computer.

The black, white, and pink blur came to a rest, and Miles saw a mysterious-looking girl in a spider-themed hoodie, wearing a mask. She webbed Miles and Peter together, hoisted the two over her shoulder, and together they swung off.

A little while later, they set down in a clearing. Doc Ock and the security guards were far behind them now. For the first time since the whole Alchemax affair started, Miles took a deep breath. He wanted to pass out and sleep for a week.

The young woman in the spider costume looked at Miles and Peter and removed her mask.

"Hey, guys," she said, smiling.

"Gwanda?" Miles asked, incredulous. She looked exactly like the new girl at Visions!

"It's Gwen, actually," she replied. "I'm from another dimension. I mean, another-another dimension."

Miles was floored. As usual, he didn't quite know what to say. So he said, "I like your haircut."

Gwen gave her hair a little flip. "You don't get to like my haircut."

The sound of gunfire echoed through the forest.

"Okay, lovebirds," Peter said. "Break it up. We've got bad guys. Everywhere o'clock."

Gwen fired her web shooter and snagged a branch. Then Peter followed suit, and they both swung away.

Miles attempted to do the same thing. He fumbled a moment, until he steadied his arm and got off the shot.

"How many more Spider-People are there?" he asked, swinging away, following Gwen and Peter.

CHAPTER 18

The encounter at Alchemax had Miles rattled. It took the length of the bus ride back to Manhattan for him to comprehend Gwen's story. That she had arrived from her universe thanks to a collider incident similar to the accident that Miles had witnessed the other night. And that she had gone to Visions Academy on some instinct, where she had met Miles.

"I like the suit," Gwen said.

Miles smiled, glad that she was finally warming up to him after the whole hair incident. "Thanks," he replied.

"Kinda says, *Yeah, I don't care how I look.* You know? I think it's rad."

"I can't tell if you're being sarcastic," Miles said, legitimately puzzled.

"To be honest, I can't, either," Gwen said. "I'm still trying to work it out."

A loud snore interrupted the conversation, and Miles turned around to see Peter snoring in the seat behind them.

"Is this guy doing it for you?" Gwen asked.

Miles thought for a moment. "Yeah," he said. "I mean, he's actually kind of good."

"Because we can totally leave him," she said. Again, Miles wasn't sure if she was kidding or not.

"I can hear you," Peter said.

"I know," Gwen replied.

Miles looked up at the modest house. It was night, and they were in Queens. There were flower bouquets covering the porch.

Suddenly, all the house lights came on at once. The front door opened just a bit, and Miles could see an old woman looking out. He recognized her—he had just seen her the day before, at the chapel.

"You guys are all very sweet, but no more fans today, please," the woman said wearily.

Then the woman peered closer at Peter, Miles, and Gwen, and she looked as if a bolt of lightning had just struck her skull. Her eyes widened, and she stepped through the door and onto the porch.

"Aunt May . . ." Peter said.

"Peter . . ." Aunt May said, stunned.

"So this is going to sound crazy . . . but I'm pretty sure I'm from–"

"An alternate dimension," Aunt May finished.

"Yeah," Peter said. Miles looked at his mentor. With his mask off, Miles swore that Peter was about to cry.

"You look tired, Peter."

"I was there when it all happened," Miles said. "I am so sorry."

"And what's your name?" Aunt May asked.

"I'm Miles."

"Gwen."

"So, did Peter have a place where we could make another goober?" Miles pulled the broken override key out and showed it to Aunt May.

"Follow me," she said.

Aunt May led the three Spiders through the backyard to a garden shed.

Suddenly, Peter grew excited. "I have one of these!" he said, voice rising. "A little shed where I keep my spider-gear!"

A spider-symbol on the door began to glow, and the door opened, revealing a small space.

An elevator.

The four went inside and activated the elevator. Miles watched as the door closed, and felt the whole thing going down.

When the doors opened, Miles was in spider-heaven. It was a giant underground laboratory filled with all kinds of amazing science gear. There were places to hang out, and all kinds of photos of Spider-Man in action.

"Whoa! Dude, was yours anything like this?" Miles said.

"Mine was like his," Peter mused, "but take away the Jeep, the plane . . . Imagine it was smaller. Imagine a futon. I feel sad for this guy."

Miles laughed, and then looked around some more. There were various spider-costumes, different iterations of the classic red-and-blue outfit. May noticed Miles gawking and walked over to him.

"He always knew it wasn't an easy job," she said. "He was trying to figure out that collider thing for a long time. Black holes, dimensions—it all sounded like a lot of hooey to me, but look . . . here you all are. You and the others."

"Others?" Gwen chimed in.

That's when Miles saw them.

A man, dressed in black and white, stepping out of the shadows. Definitely a Spider.

A girl with black hair, maybe Miles's age? Jumping, hitting the ground. A strange spidery robot landing on the ground right behind her.

A . . . pig?

"My name is Peter Parker," said the Spider in black and white.

"My name is Peni Parker," said the girl. She jerked her thumb toward the robot that followed closely behind her. "This is SP//dr."

"My name is Peter Porker," snorted the pig. "Also known as Spider-Ham."

"In my universe, it's 1938," said the black-and-white Peter.

"In my universe, it's the year 3145," said the girl.

"Okay. Let me guess," Gwen said, trying to bring some organization to all the chaos. "Out of nowhere, you all got sucked out of your own dimension."

Everyone nodded. Then Miles gasped as both Peter Porker and the black-and-white Spider glitched.

"Well, this just got way more—" Peter began, before glitching again. "Complicated."

"If you're all here and you're all like that . . . my job just got a whole lot harder," Miles said. "All your universes, they're in danger, too. If I can't finish what Peter started, your home, my home, they'll all be gone."

The Spider-Man in black turned to Miles. "Who are you again?" he asked.

Peter stepped up. "This is Miles. He's going to save the multiverse."

The pig looked Miles up and down, then stared at Peter. "How is he going to do that?"

"We worked it out," Peter replied.

We did? Miles thought.

CHAPTER 19

Miles lost track of time. They had been in Peter's—the other Peter's—secret hideout/lab for who knows, an hour? Two hours? More?

The whole time, the Spiders were offering Miles advice on how to use his powers. Do this, do that, try this, try that. It was too much all at once, coming at him from all sides. He'd had his spider-powers only a few short days, and now so much was resting on his thirteen-year-old shoulders.

Nothing big, Miles thought. *Just the fate of the world.*

Merely watching these individuals from different dimensions coming together for a common purpose—to stop Fisk and save their universes—made Miles feel like . . . like . . .

. . . maybe he wasn't worthy. Maybe he couldn't hack it.

So when he thought no one was watching, he walked over to the elevator and got in.

Maybe I just need some fresh air.

Or maybe . . . maybe I just need to walk away from all this.

The elevator door opened, and Miles walked out into the cold night air. He took a deep breath and looked around May's tiny backyard.

What am I doing? I can't do this. There's no way. I can't do this.

"What's with your, you know . . . feelings?" asked a voice from behind.

Peter.

"I'm not like you guys. I can't do this," Miles said. It all seemed so hopeless. He sounded and felt defeated.

"Look, kid, you gotta help me out here."

"*I* gotta help *you*?" Miles asked in disbelief.

"Yeah," Peter said. "I mean, this is new to me. I'm not the mentor type. I'm thirty-eight years old, and I've barely figured this Spider-Man stuff out myself."

Miles paused. "I'm supposed to save the world, Peter."

"Well, there's your problem. You can't think about saving the whole world. You have to think about saving *one person*, Miles. You just think about someone you love."

"My mom and my uncle and my dad."

Peter thought for a second. "In that order? Want to talk about that?"

Miles shook his head. "No."

"Technically, that's more than one person, but I'll give it to you. The thing is, this hero business? It gets really, really complicated, man. You lose things."

"But it's worth it, right?" Miles asked.

"I hope so."

"How do I know I won't fail?"

"You won't," Peter said, smiling. "It's a leap of faith. In the end, that's all it is, Miles. A leap of faith. That's all I got."

With that, Peter headed back inside the spider-den. Miles was alone for a moment and felt his phone vibrate. He pulled it out and looked at the screen. Two missed calls from his mom. When he swiped away the notification, he saw the wallpaper on his phone.

It was a picture of the mural that he and his uncle Aaron had painted, just the other night.

He needed someone to talk to. Someone who wouldn't judge him, who would just listen. Someone who wouldn't try to give him all this advice about what he should be doing with his powers.

Uncle Aaron, he thought. *I need to see Uncle Aaron.*

Miles realized that he must have known it subconsciously,

because he had been heading toward his uncle's place the whole time. With his newfound powers, Miles scaled his uncle's building and came to rest on the fire escape outside his window. Taking a deep breath, he opened the window and climbed inside.

"Uncle Aaron?" Miles called out. But there was no answer. Of course. Miles shook his head in disgust at his own vacant-headedness. He'd known Uncle Aaron would still be out of town. This Super Hero stuff must be messing with his brain even more than he'd thought.

The phone started to ring, and Miles waited for the machine to pick up. He heard his uncle's taped message. Then a familiar voice:

"Aaron, it's Jeff. I need you to call me if you've heard from Miles. He has a soft spot for you, and he's missing. You know I wouldn't reach out if this wasn't important. Thanks."

Dad.

Not knowing what else to do, Miles searched his uncle's kitchen for a pad of paper and a pen. Then he started to write a note.

Uncle Aaron:
I have to do something very deadly. If something happens, please tell my parents bye.
    P.S. I am Spi

Before he could finish the note, he heard a noise on the fire escape. Then the burning, buzzing sensation at the base of his skull.

Danger?

Miles saw a silhouette moving closer, coming toward the window. He recognized its shape instantly.

The Prowler.

What is the Prowler doing here?!

That nervous feeling welled up in his stomach, and as Miles looked to the window, he saw something strange.

Rather, he *didn't* see something strange.

He didn't see his hand.

He had become invisible again.

"Yes, hello, Mr. Fisk," the Prowler said into his phone. "I've got the security tapes from the tunnel right here. If the kid's out there, I'll find him."

The Prowler was now inside the apartment, inches away from the invisible Miles. When he took off his mask, it took all of Miles's willpower not to scream out.

The Prowler was Uncle Aaron.

"You know me, sir," he said into the phone. "I don't ever quit."

Despite himself, Miles gasped.

Uncle Aaron's head snapped in Miles's direction. He put his mask back on.

Miles, still invisible, backed toward the window. The Prowler must have noticed him, somehow, because he followed.

In a flash, Miles was out the window, dropping down, now completely visible.

With the Prowler hot on his tail.

CHAPTER 20

"**T**he goober is ready!" Peni said with a note of triumph in her voice.

She had been working at the computer in the living room, right alongside Aunt May, when the front door burst open.

"My uncle!"

Miles barely got the words out of his mouth as he stumbled inside. He was gasping for air, and he felt as if he was going to hurl. He hadn't slowed his pace since he split from his uncle's apartment. After all, the Prowler was probably right behind him, and Miles was terrified that he would follow him wherever he went. But he had nowhere else to go, and he knew it.

It was all too much, and he couldn't handle it alone.

"Hey, where have you been?" Peter asked. "We–"

"My uncle Aaron, he–he–he's the Prowler! He works for Fisk. . . . He tried to kill me!"

Looking up, Miles saw the Spiders from different universes surrounding him, all ready for action, all ready to help him.

"Were you followed?" Gwen asked.

"No," Miles said with a swagger he didn't feel.

I hope I lost the Prowler. I'm pretty sure I lost him. Like, sixty percent sure? Forty-five percent?

Then the thought hit him.

What if I didn't lose him at all?

Miles didn't have long to wait for his answer. The floor shook, and metallic tentacles smashed through the wall. Drywall and wood exploded everywhere as Doc Ock entered the living room. She was flanked by Tombstone and another tentacled villain–the Scorpion.

"Okay," Miles said. "I guess I was followed."

"I think I'll be taking that," Doc Ock said, gesturing at Peter. Miles looked at Peter's hands and saw him clutching the new override key that he had made.

Then the Scorpion leaped in front of Miles, blocking his path. Without even thinking, Miles grabbed something to defend himself with. Unfortunately, it turned out to be couch cushions.

"¿Estás listo?" the Scorpion said. "Dale niñito."

"¡Prepárate, que te vas a morir!" Miles replied.

Before the Scorpion could attack, Peni executed a perfect backflip into the SP//dr armor. SP//dr smashed through the ceiling.

Ock's tentacles reached out to grab the drive. As Peter engaged the enemy, he tossed the drive to the black-and-white Spider-Man.

Another tentacle reached out, trying to squash him. Then the black-and-white Spider tossed the drive to the pig in the Spider-Suit.

Tombstone picked up a couch and threw it at Gwen. She ducked it, webbed it, and threw it right back at Tombstone. It knocked the big bruiser into—and through—the front window.

In a matter of seconds, the battle spilled out from Aunt May's house and into the neighborhood beyond. The Spiders drew Doc Ock, Tombstone, and the Scorpion outside. Miles could hear Ock was screaming desperately for the USB drive.

Which Miles saw lying in a pile of debris on the living room floor.

Who dropped it? he wondered. *Doesn't matter. Gotta grab it!*

Miles was in the middle of snatching the drive off the

floor, when he felt the burning sensation at the back of his neck. He whirled around, only to find himself face-to-face with the Prowler.

"Don't be stupid, kid," the Prowler said, flashing his claws, swiping at Miles.

Sprinting upstairs, Miles tried to get away from his uncle. But the Prowler grabbed his leg, pulling him down. Miles kicked and got the Prowler off him.

He raced upstairs, where he found a giant hole in the roof.

SP//dr must have made it when Peni blasted out of here, he thought.

Miles jumped through the hole and spun a web. But before he could swing away, the Prowler had leaped onto the roof, blocking his path.

"Nowhere left to run!" the Prowler said. "Hand it over, now!"

Miles's heart was racing. He could hear his pulse inside his ears. He could think of only one thing to do.

He took off his mask.

The Prowler staggered back. "Miles?" he said.

"Uncle Aaron," he said. Miles was trembling.

Then the Prowler took off his mask. "Oh, no, no, no, no," Uncle Aaron said.

"Prowler, what are you waiting for? End him. Or I will!"

Miles looked at the ground below and saw Wilson Fisk standing there. Waiting. Waiting for his uncle to do the unthinkable.

"Please, Uncle Aaron," Miles begged.

Uncle Aaron looked at his nephew and slowly, slightly, lowered his claws.

A gunshot rang out.

Fisk.

Miles felt his body pushed aside as his uncle grabbed him, shoving him to the roof.

His uncle took the bullet meant for him.

Miles couldn't move—he couldn't believe what was happening. He saw Peter swinging in below, slamming into Fisk, knocking him to the ground. He heard Peter yell something at him, but he couldn't process it.

It was all he could do to scoop up his uncle in his arms and web-swing away from May's house.

CHAPTER 21

The alley was dark.

As dark as Miles's mood.

"Miles . . ." Uncle Aaron groaned.

"Uncle Aaron. This is my fault," he said as he kneeled down over his uncle.

"No, Miles," his uncle said, trying hard to breathe. "I'm sorry. I wanted you to look up to me. I let you down, man, I let you down. You're the best of all of us, Miles. You're on your way. Just . . . keep going . . . just keep going. . . ."

Miles was in tears, sobbing, but no sound came.

He hugged his uncle, their faces pressed together. Miles couldn't feel his uncle's breath anymore.

"Hands up!"

Miles didn't have to turn around. He recognized the voice, knew it better than his own.

His dad.

"Put your arms up now! Turn around!"

Reflexively, Miles went invisible. His father ran over, baffled by what just happened.

Jefferson looked at the ground, and it was clear that he recognized the lifeless body lying there.

"Aaron? Aaron. No . . ." he said, voice cracking. He leaned down and touched his brother's face.

Jefferson grabbed his shoulder radio and set his jaw. "All units. I want an APB on a new Spider-Man."

Miles raced through the hallway of his dorm, heading right for his room. He grabbed the doorknob, flung the door open, and nearly tore the thing off its hinges. Then he slammed it shut, and the plaster around the door frame cracked.

"It's all my fault!" Miles yelled as he shoved all the homework and stacks of books that he had piled on his desk. They hit the floor, spilling everywhere. Then he knocked over a chair and watched as it splintered into pieces.

It was as if he didn't know his own strength.

And he didn't care.

All he knew was that his uncle was dead, and he felt

responsible, somehow. And now his own dad wanted to catch Miles, like Miles was some kind of criminal.

"Hey, bud, you okay?"

Miles looked up and saw Peter poking his head into the dorm window. Then the black-and-white Spider, the pig, Peni, and Gwen.

"We've all been there," Peter said, his voice suddenly gentle. "For me, it was Uncle Ben."

The black-and-white Spider spoke softly. "For me, it was Uncle Benjamin."

"For me, it was my father," Peni said solemnly.

"For me, it was my best friend," Gwen added.

"For me . . . it was when my uncle was killed in front of me. Uncle Frank Furter. He was electrocuted. It smelled so good."

The pig said that.

"It was my fault. You wouldn't understand," Miles said.

"Miles, we're probably the only ones who *do* understand," Gwen said, trying to soothe Miles.

She's right. I know she's right.

Miles had so many feelings racing around him, the only thing that he knew for sure was that he had to do something. He had all these powers, could do all these amazing things–and he had to use them for something. Something good.

We gotta get you guys home, Miles thought.

But when he turned to look at his fellow Spiders, he saw only Gwen climbing out the window and Peter remaining in the room. The others had already left.

"What's going on?" Miles said, clutching the override key.

"Bye, Miles," Gwen said, her voice low.

"Miles," Peter said, his voice halting. "I came to say good-bye."

"We can say good-bye at the collider!"

"You're staying here."

"I need to be there," Miles said, practically begging. "So you can all go home!"

"They are going home," Peter said. "I'm the only one staying."

"You're taking my place?" Miles asked, incredulous.

"Not everything works out, kid," Peter said. "I need the goober. Please don't make me take it from you."

"That's not fair," Miles protested. "You've gotta tell them I can do this!" He glared at Peter, and it became instantly clear that this wasn't a group decision. Peter, and Peter alone, had decided.

"It was my call, Miles."

Miles took a step forward, closing the distance between him and Peter. "I gotta make Fisk pay! You have to let me make him pay! I'm ready! I promise!"

In a blur, Peter nearly knocked Miles to the floor, catching him at the last second. "Then venom-strike me right now. Or turn invisible on command so you can get past me."

From deep within, Miles struggled to do either of those things. But it wasn't happening. He hated himself for it.

"Look, I know how much you want this, kid," Peter said, trying to console Miles. "But you don't have it."

Before he could do anything, Peter webbed a desk chair underneath Miles and gave it a spin, wrapping the teenager in a cocoon. Then Peter took the override key.

"I'm sorry, but it has to be me," Peter said sadly. He couldn't even look at Miles.

"Peter, listen to me—" Miles started to say.

Then Peter webbed his mouth shut.

"Now you don't have to be Spider-Man," Peter said, and he jumped through the window, swinging away into the night.

He was so deep in self-pity that he didn't even hear the knocking at first. But then it came again, insistent.

KNOCK, KNOCK, KNOCK.

Miles rolled the chair over to the door, and then he heard the voice.

"Miles! Miles, it's your dad! I've been looking for you. Please open the door."

Slowly, Miles rolled the chair away from the door, an inch at a time, quiet as he could.

"Miles, I can see your shadow moving around."

Miles stopped in his tracks.

"Yeah. Okay, I get it. I get it. Still ignoring me," Jefferson said. "Look, can we talk for a minute? Something happened to . . . Sometimes people drift apart, Miles. Even when they don't want to. I . . . I don't want that to happen to us."

Listening to his dad through the door, Miles thought he was going to cry all over again.

"Look, I know I don't always do what you need me to do, or say what you need me to say, but . . . I see this . . . this spark in you. It's amazing, and it's why I push you. But it's yours, and whatever you choose to do with it, you'll be great."

Miles wanted to say something, but he couldn't.

"I know I said you don't have a choice, but you do. Look, call me when you can, okay?" Jefferson finished. "I love you. You don't have to say it back, though."

Then he heard his father's footsteps as Jefferson walked back down the hall.

Closing his eyes, Miles concentrated, and his hands started to crackle with energy. It was his venom strike—and he was in full control. The charge surged outward, frying the webbing, freeing Miles from his bonds.

122

CHAPTER 22

Something was wrong.

Where were the Spiders?

Miles had made his way back to the subway tunnel where it all began just a few days ago. He knew the precise location of Fisk's supercollider and was prepared to do whatever it would take to stop the machine from destroying his world, along with countless others.

But to do it, he would need the Spiders' help. He assumed they would be here already. But there was no sign of them. Just a bunch of Fisk's men guarding the fence. And near them, a few cans of spray paint that Miles and his uncle had left behind the other night.

Why aren't they here already? Miles thought. *Did Fisk get them?*

One of the men said, "Let's finish it up, huh?" and grabbed a can of spray paint. Then he started to add on to the mural.

It made Miles sick to see something that he and his uncle had created together defiled like that.

In his invisible state, it was a simple matter for Miles to climb the fence and move down the tunnel, completely unseen. He watched as the guard spray-painted *Ronald* onto the mural.

That was it.

The invisible Spider grabbed the can from the man's hand and, in a flash, became visible. He threw the man toward the fence and hit him with a venom strike. Fisk's goon shuddered, then slammed into the fence, his electrified body electrifying the fence itself. The men who were leaning up against the fence all received a hefty jolt and dropped to the ground, groaning.

Once again invisible, Miles continued his crawl, sneaking past Fisk's armed guards, as well as the Scorpion.

Initiating secondary ignition cycle.

Miles recognized the voice instantly as the computer that controlled the collider.

Gotta hurry, or it's all gonna be over. Like, really *over.*

Scampering along the top of the tunnel, he found

a hatch that had survived the previous explosion in the chamber and pried it open with his sticky fingers. Then he crawled inside.

A few seconds later, he found another hatch, and Miles popped it open and dropped to the ground below. He was inside the collider room.

And so were the Spiders.

They were all there already, but they were glitching. Badly. Miles could see them as they crawled along the ceiling.

Opening detected, came the voice from the computer. *Aperture at zero point forty-two micrometers and counting.*

The room quaked, and Miles could only imagine the damage that was bleeding out across the city.

Miles watched as a portal began to grow, larger and larger, pulsing with energy. Then came the computer voice once more: *Quantum entanglement is engaged.*

What are they entangling? Miles thought. *Or . . . whom?*

Miles watched as Peter reached the control panel and produced the override key he had taken from Miles. He was just about to insert it, when four metallic tentacles pried open a gaping hole in the ceiling.

Doc Ock.

"Nice to see you again, Peter," Doc Ock said sarcastically.

Her tentacles whipped out, slamming into Peter. The other Spiders jumped to his aid, but by now, Fisk's goons had assembled and were firing their weapons at the Spiders. They should have been able to fight them off with ease, but all the glitching—which had only grown worse—was making it next to impossible.

"It's an ambush!" Gwen shouted, swinging in to fight Doc Ock. Swatting her away with a tentacle, Doc Ock pressed her attack on Peter.

Miles knew that he had to keep his presence hidden until the last possible second. If he was going to have any hope of surviving this, of sending the Spiders home, and saving the world, Miles—all of them—had to play it right.

He spun a web and caught Gwen on her way down. She didn't see Miles, he was sure of it.

Then Miles looked up to see Peter struggling against Doc Ock.

"I told you I wanted to watch," Doc Ock said, gloating. "Good-bye, Peter Parker!" Then she picked up Peter with her tentacles and threw him into the beam that was projecting the portal.

Then Miles sprang into action. He jumped up from the ground, spun a web, and swung in, catching Peter and pulling him away.

"Did I teach you that?" Peter said.

126

Miles stuck the landing and set Peter down, just as Doc Ock began her attack anew. The two Spiders stood side by side, using their powers to evade their enemy. A tentacle *whoosh*ed right above Miles's head, but he ducked it with ease.

I might just be getting the hang of this Spider-Man thing. . . .

Warning: maximum tolerance exceeded, came the voice from the computer. *Warning: maximum tolerance exceeded.*

That can't be good. . . .

CHAPTER 23

"Whoa boy!" said the pig.

"This is bad!" Miles agreed. The whole collider room had been thrown into chaos. The portal was steadily growing now, the quakes getting worse and worse. Inside the portal, Miles could now see objects appearing. Buildings?

"But weirdly, kind of cool," Peter said, studying the phenomenon before them.

Before anyone could say another word, a car flew out of the portal, nearly taking off the black-and-white Spider's head. Next was a streetlight. Then a hot-dog cart.

In between dodging the various objects that had now begun to stream in through the portal, the Spiders continued their battle against Fisk's guards. SP//dr and the pig were keeping the Scorpion occupied, while Gwen set down in front of Doc Ock.

"Let's dance," Miles heard Gwen say as the two began to tangle. Gwen took a swing at Doc Ock, but she was batted away by one of her tentacles. Gwen was caught a second later by both Miles and Peter, who had spun a web basket to catch her and fling her right back at Doc Ock.

Gwen kicked Doc Ock square in the chest, knocking her backward toward the portal.

That's when the doctor was smashed by an eighteen-wheeler that was careening through the portal.

"Time to shut this baby down!" Peter said.

Surprised he didn't say It's go time.

"I got it, guys," Miles said. Then he showed Peter the override key in his hand.

"Oh, you gotta be kidding!" Peter said. "When did you get that?"

"Don't watch the mouth," Miles said, throwing Peter's words back at him. "Watch the hands!"

Then Miles went into action. He leaped into the air, spinning a web and swinging, then hit the wall and began to crawl. Then he flipped and, in a flash, was at the control panel. He ripped it off as if it were paper.

"I love this kid," Peter said.

Inside, Miles saw a slot. He slid in the override key, and turned; it was a perfect fit.

Alert, said the computer voice. *Quantum polarity has been reversed.*

"He did it!" Peni shouted. "We're going home!"

The portal was still active, even though Miles had reversed the polarity. He still needed to shut the thing down, or the quakes would continue, and destruction would reign.

"You guys have to go now," Miles said. "I gotta destroy this thing."

Before it destroys everything else.

"Miles, are you sure?" Gwen said, uncertain.

"What about Fisk?" Peter asked.

"There's still plenty of bad guys," the pig added.

"Guys! I'm Spider-Man!" Miles said, sounding confident for the first time.

"Okay, peace out!" the pig said, and he jumped into the portal.

He agreed to that a little fast, Miles thought, chuckling to himself.

One by one, Miles looked at the remaining Spiders, and they at him.

"Arigato, Miles!" Peni said as SP//dr jumped into the portal.

She was followed by the black-and-white Spider. "I love you all," he said, choked up, and Miles was amazed. Then the black-and-white Spider jumped through the portal, too.

Miles turned to face Gwen. He didn't know what to say.

"Do I get to like your hairdo now?" Miles said.

Gwen laughed. "I like your suit. It fits you."

"I can't tell if you're being sarcastic. . . ."

"I'm not making fun of you," Gwen said. "You're my friend. See you around."

They smiled at each other as Gwen jumped into the portal.

That left only Peter.

"Your turn."

"I don't know what to say. But . . . thanks," Peter said, fumbling for words.

Miles heard a crash, and looked over to see Fisk climbing out of the smashed window of the collider control room.

"I'll hold him off," Peter said. "You go destroy this thing. It's okay, kid." He sounded resigned to his fate, as if he were willing to make the ultimate sacrifice to save everyone.

"Yeah," Miles agreed. "It is okay."

And Miles drop-kicked Peter, catching him completely off guard, and dangled him over the portal.

"This will all make you a better Peter Parker," Miles said, and dropped him into the portal.

As Peter disappeared through the portal, Miles could hear him say, "Go get 'em, kid."

CHAPTER 24

The enormous portal was growing out of control, and assorted objects were now appearing at random inside the chamber, objects from different universes. Pieces of concrete, street signs, a taxi filled with frightened people, chunks of a bridge—it was all swirling around inside the chamber.

Fisk was down there, waiting, waiting.

Miles got caught up in all the confusion, knocked about as the dimensions crossed over. The next thing he knew, Miles was picking himself up off the floor of a subway car. Fisk was there, and he started throwing punches at Miles.

Fisk hit him again. And again. Miles tried to stop him, but it was no use—Fisk was fighting like a man possessed.

And then Fisk stopped fighting altogether.

Miles, dazed, looked up and saw a young man and an older woman walking through the train car.

"Vanessa!" Fisk shouted. "Richard!"

"Dad?" the man called.

"Wilson?" the woman asked.

"Vanessa, it's me!" Fisk said, overcome with emotion.

The woman looked bewildered. "What's happening?"

"It's all right, you're home!" Fisk yelled.

But something wasn't right. The woman held on to the young man. "Stay back!" she said, anger in her voice. "Stay away from us!"

"Don't go!" Fisk pleaded. "Stay with me!"

Fury filling his eyes, Fisk lashed out at Miles again, pummeling him with crushing blows.

"You can't bring them back!" Miles roared, realizing now exactly what Fisk had been trying to do all along. Bring back his lost family—plucking them from another dimension to live with him here in this one.

"Watch me!" Fisk thundered, striking Miles again and again.

Miles was delirious. At the last second, he turned his head, only to see Fisk coming right at him with a steel beam. It slammed into his head, rattling his brain, knocking him to the ground.

Then the whole train car started to spin, and Miles

glanced outside through the window. Inexplicably, they were hurtling toward the Brooklyn Bridge. The car smashed into the concrete, rolling, sending Miles and Fisk tumbling about.

A moment later, Miles, shaken, found himself back in the collider chamber, thrown from the train car. He ripped off his mask as he got to his feet. Then the train doors burst open as Fisk appeared, charging right for Miles.

Fisk threw punch after punch after punch, each one finding its mark.

But still Miles stood his ground.

"What else you got?" Miles said, gazing directly into Fisk's eyes. He waited, waited for Fisk to recognize him.

And he did.

"I see the family resemblance," Fisk sneered. "But your uncle can't save you now, can he?"

"He doesn't have to," Miles said defiantly. "I learned a lot from my uncle. You ever hear of the shoulder touch?"

"What?" Fisk said.

Before Fisk could do anything, Miles dropped a hand on his shoulder, said, "Hey," and unleashed a full-force venom strike.

In the distance, he could see Doc Ock, scrambling, looking around wildly. Miles thought about going after her, but before he could do anything, she jumped through the portal.

It's go time.

Miles slammed the button on the control panel, the one that would shut down everything.

And almost instantaneously, it did exactly that.

The collider switched off, and the shaking in the chamber stopped.

The computer voice said, *Unit functions are terminal. Unit functions are terminal.*

Miles slumped down, exhausted.

EPILOGUE

Miles picked up the phone. He just wanted to go back to his bed and sleep, but there was something he had to do. He was crouched atop a building, looking down below as he saw a police cruiser outside the subway stop. It was his dad's car. Jefferson was inside the car, probably doing paperwork. Cops had to do a lot of paperwork.

He hit the DIAL button on his phone and put it to his ear.

It rang once.

"Miles! Are you okay?" Jefferson said into the receiver.

"Yeah, I'm okay," Miles said, exhausted but trying to sound casual. "You're probably busy, so–"

"No, no, no, no, I can talk!" Jefferson said. He sounded

glad to know his son was all right. "I can talk. So I came by earlier because your uncle . . ."

"I know, Dad. I'm so sorry," Miles said softly.

"Yeah, me too. What I said at the door, it wasn't just talk."

"Sure, Dad. I'm glad you're okay. I need to go," Miles said.

"Look, you know, I was thinking maybe we could find a nice wall, privately owned, like at the police station–" Jefferson began.

"Dad, I–"

"–and you could . . . throw up some of your art?"

"I really need to go, so . . . talk later, bye!" Miles said, hanging up the phone.

His dad was still talking when Miles pulled down his Spider-Man mask and leaped down to the street below, landing next to the police cruiser.

"Officer?" he said.

"Spider-Man?" Jefferson said, startled. "Hey, listen. I owe you an a–"

Then Spider-Man hugged Jefferson.

"I look forward to working with you," he said to his father.

"Me too, I guess," Jefferson said, clearly bewildered.

"Thank you for your bravery tonight. I love you," Spider-Man said.

Jefferson looked at the web-slinger and said, "Wait, what?"

Then Spider-Man spun a web and swung off into the night as he shouted, "And look behind you!"

Just like that, Spider-Man was gone. Jefferson turned around and saw Fisk webbed to a lamppost. Jefferson walked, then ran, over to the unconscious criminal. When he got there, he saw a small piece of paper stuck to Fisk's chest that simply read,

FROM YOUR FRIENDLY NEIGHBORHOOD
SPIDER-MAN.